Theodore Goodridge Roberts

THE
HARBOR
MASTER

Introduction: DESMOND PACEY

General Editor: MALCOLM ROSS

NEW CANADIAN LIBRARY NO. 63

MCCLELLAND AND STEWART LIMITED

The Canadian Publishers
McClelland and Stewart Limited,
25 Hollinger Road, Toronto 16

PRINTED AND BOUND IN ENGLAND BY
HAZELL WATSON AND VINEY LTD
AYLESBURY, BUCKS

Contents

∞ *Introduction*

I WELL REMEMBER my first glimpse of Theodore
Goodridge Roberts. It was in October of 1944,
and "Thede," as everyone called him, had
recently returned to live in Fredericton, as he had been returning off and on through the years. His stay was a relatively brief
one, but in the next few months, before he moved to Digby,
Nova Scotia, I came to know him well. He was a striking figure
as he strode up and down University Avenue: he was tall,
slim, and held himself erect with a bearing that suggested his
military training and his strict code of honor; he was dressed,
invariably as I recall him, in grey – a light grey flannel suit in
Fall and Spring, a grey overcoat with a fur collar in Winter; his
face was thin, the skin almost transparent and very pale yellow
in hue, his hair white and fine; but in contrast with the prevail-
ing paleness were his dark brown eyes, which shone with an
eager glow. His alert eyes suggested vitality and curiosity, an
appetite for experience which his dress and relaxed manner did
their futile best to belie.

What impressed me most about Thede's personality was his
courtesy and generosity. I was a young and very inexperienced
professor at that time, but Thede always treated me as if I were
a proven scholar and a sophisticated man of the world. He took
you at your best, and had the knack of making you feel at your
best. His manners were those of a gentleman of the old school:
there was a true courtliness about him, a grace of movement
and gesture, a gentleness of speech and a quiet friendliness. His
generosity manifested itself in several ways: in his readiness to
read his poems, without any suggestion of payment, to university students or to gatherings in the Observatory Art Centre on
Sunday afternoons; in his willingness to advise me and other
apprentice writers about the methods of publication and the
ways of publishers and editors; in the way he gave his friendship immediately and unconditionally, making you feel that
you were placed forever within his circle of trust.

And his generosity will always be especially associated in
my mind with the last time I saw him. It was in February of

1949, and I was travelling to Acadia University for the meeting of a committee. I let Thede know that I should be in Digby on the way to and from Acadia, and although he was then over seventy and suffering from the heart trouble that was four years later to take his life, he insisted on meeting me at the Digby boat on my journey over, and on seeing me off on the boat on my journey back. For the return journey, a heavy sea was running and it was obvious that the crossing would be a rough one. Just before the boat sailed, Thede turned to me and said, "Here's something that will make the crossing bearable. Drink this, and I guarantee you won't be sick!" – and he handed me a pint bottle of rum. I knew that Thede at that time was desperately poor, and was eking out a precarious existence by selling adventure stories to the pulps, and this knowledge made his gift all the more admirable. It would have been unthinkable to refuse it.

The qualities in Theodore Roberts which I have tried to sketch are reflected in the novel which follows. There is his vividness of perception in the sensory details, which give to the otherwise somewhat melodramatic story its air of authenticity; his code of honor, against which all the men are measured, and according to which all the women are treated; his optimism about human nature, which leads him eventually to redeem even the villainous Black Dennis Nolan; and his generosity of spirit, which leads him to suggest, against the laws of probability, that even Nolan would be ready to give part of his dubious wealth to the building of a church.

∽

George Edward Theodore Roberts (he afterwards changed his name to Theodore Goodridge Roberts in tribute to his older brother Goodridge, who died young) was born on July 7, 1877 in the red-brick rectory on George Street in Fredericton, New Brunswick. He was the fourth son and fifth and last child of the Reverend George Goodridge Roberts, Rector of St. Ann's Parish and Canon of Christ Church Cathedral. When Theodore was three years old his eldest brother Charles published *Orion*, the book of poetry that ushered in the first movement of truly Canadian verse, and so it is not surprising that from boyhood days Theodore also thought of writing as a possible career. His first poem was published in *The Independent*, a New York literary magazine briefly edited by his cousin Bliss Carman, when he was only eleven years old. About the same time, in the late eighteen-eighties, he had two eerie short stories accepted by unidentified American magazines. Thus began a long and productive literary career which saw Theodore publish thirty-four novels, four books of verse, and well over a hundred short stories.

Roberts was educated at the Fredericton Collegiate School, where his grandfather had been headmaster for forty years, and at the University of New Brunswick, where his grandfather had been for a brief period professor of Greek. He did not complete the degree course at U.N.B., however, but instead dropped out to try his hand at farming near Stanley, and after a year or so – in the summer of 1897 – went to New York as sub-editor of *The Independent*. For that magazine he went, in 1898, to Florida and Cuba as a correspondent from the Spanish-American War, but contracted malaria and returned to Fredericton for a year or so to recuperate. From 1899 to 1902 he lived in Newfoundland, editing *The Newfoundland Magazine* and free-lancing, and it was the knowledge of Newfoundland life which he gained during these three years that he drew upon to write *The Harbor Master*. There followed a few months at sea, a brief stay in New York, and a second return to Fredericton, where, in November, 1903, he married Frances Seymour Allen, a nurse and the daughter of the Methodist minister in Elgin, New Brunswick. The honeymoon was spent in Barbados, where the Roberts' lived for the next two years and where their son Goodridge, now the well-known Canadian painter, was born on September 24, 1904. After the Barbados interval came a third return to Fredericton. Thus the pattern of Theodore's life was established: a few months or years elsewhere – in England, France, Ottawa or Digby – would be followed by a return to Fredericton, which was always the hub of his life's wheel.

The last return occurred in February, 1953. Theodore had died at Digby on Tuesday, February 24, and on Saturday, February 28 he was buried in Fredericton's Forest Hill Cemetery, near the graves of his brother Charles G. D. Roberts, and his cousin Bliss Carman.

 හහ

The Harbor Master (which was published in England under the title of *The Toll of the Tides*) was written in Fredericton in

1911, during one of Theodore's most productive periods, and was published in London in 1912, and in Boston in 1913. Roberts had returned from France to Fredericton in 1911, and from then until the outbreak of World War I he averaged three novels a year. On its original publication, the novel was well received by the critics. *The Nation* (London), for example, in its issue of February 15, 1913, declared: "We have the reality of life, the drenching of seas, the destructive force of the winds ... [It] is a strong book," and the reviewer in *The Spectator* wrote (on February 8, 1913):

> He gives us a most vigorous and graphic story of a brief enterprise of organized wrecking, and there is more in it than mere excitement and violence. There is plenty of those, and one gruesome touch besides, but underneath is the more subtle effect wrought by a new lust of gold upon the characters of the men and of the community as a whole. Mr. Roberts does not insist on the moral, any more than on the superstitions of the older folk, that some things which come from the sea are the gifts of the saints and others of the devil; but none the less we learn the law that food and gear are fair toll from the sea to eke out a bitterly hard life: gold, jewels and women are not.

Readers of this edition will, I trust, agree that the novel has worn well, and that it deserves the place usually accorded it as the most authentic and soundly constructed of all Theodore Roberts' novels.

The Harbor Master belongs, of course, to a tradition which was a potent one at its date of composition but is now out of critical favor. The tradition went back to Sir Walter Scott and had included, in the nineteenth century, Alexandre Dumas, Wilkie Collins, Charles Dickens and Robert Louis Stevenson, as well as such Canadians as Gilbert Parker, William Kirby and Agnes Laut. There were differences of stature and attitude among these writers, but they were all agreed on certain essentials: that a novel should have a strong and intricate plot, that it should contain striking and deliberately contrasting characters, that it should have a setting remote or exotic either in space or time, that it should create an atmosphere of suspenseful apprehension, and that in the end the apprehensions should be relieved and the harmony of men and nature restored.

Of this not undistinguished and recently unjustly despised tradition *The Harbor Master* is a good if not a superlative example. It is written, obviously, by a professional, by one who knows how to set his scene and introduce his characters in such a way as to enlist our interest and arouse our suspense. When one reads the opening paragraphs, one is struck by their sensory accuracy, and is reminded that their author was also the author of perhaps the most brilliantly precise descriptive and atmospheric poem in Canadian verse, "The Blue Heron." Roberts' power to "make us see" (in Conrad's phrase) is, indeed, his greatest gift as a novelist : over and over again he gives reality to his story by inserting accurate touches of descriptive detail :

> Snow lay in patches over the bleak and sodden barren, a raw wind beat in from the east, and a gray and white sea snarled below.

ॐ

> The curtained bed was a mass of gloom; a white Christ on a cross of ebony gleamed above the narrow chimney-shelf, between two candlesticks of dull brass; the floor, with its few rough mats, was as cold as the frozen snow outside.

ॐ

> The dawn was lifting by now, clear, glass-gray and narrow at the rim of the sea to the eastward and southward. The air was still. The lapping of the tide along the icy land-wash and the dull whispering of it among the seaward rocks were the only sounds.

The best example of all, of course, is the brilliant and eerie passage in Chapter VII, which describes the emergence of the dead woman from the flooded cabin of the wrecked ship.

The descriptive passages are not merely ornamental – indeed they are rarely ornamental at all since the setting of the novel, as befits its theme, is bleak and rugged – but play their part in creating the atmosphere and reinforcing the theme. The passage about the dead woman, for example, forms a sort of objective correlative of the whole plot, gives visible presence to the poisonous atmosphere created by Nolan's greed, and epitomizes the horror of his undertakings. It is in this capacity to find tangible equivalents for emotions and ideas that Roberts at his best approaches such of his masters as Scott, Dickens and Stevenson.

Roberts also approaches greatness in his powers of characterization. From the very moment of his appearance Black Dennis Nolan arouses our curiosity. He is presented to us at first as merely a tyrant, his only redeeming feature being physical courage; but as the novel proceeds we gradually become aware of subtler and more positive qualities in him – he is "ambitious . . . imaginative, daring . . . full of resources and energy," tender towards women and children, respectful of Father McQueen, "could master himself as well as others," charitable towards his neighbours – until his final redemption seems credible and even inevitable. There is, in other words, genuine character development.

The other main triumph of characterization is Mother Nolan, a figure who in her superstitions and ominous utterances might have come from the pages of Sir Walter Scott were she not also so convincingly a woman of the Newfoundland outports. The other inhabitants of the outport are also well done, but the characters from "up-along," Flora Lockhart and Jack Darling especially, are paste-board figures of romance. There was a vein of artistic irresponsibility in Roberts, which led him to squander his very real gifts on novels of which the great majority are mere pot-boilers, and which allows him even in *The Harbor Master* to dilute his strongly created characters with persons who have no depth or complexity.

A similarly mixed verdict must be returned in respect to the plot. Although the main plot is well handled, and the three subplots are cleverly interwoven with it, there are some touches of awkwardness in the narration, as if Roberts were too lazy or too careless to seek perfection. If we prize narrative dexterity, our heart sinks when we read such sentences as "Now we must look around for Dick Lynch, who did not go out of this history when he departed so boldly from Chance Along with his sealing-gun on his shoulder," or such lame explanations as "The skipper had returned to the harbor because the ship in distress had drifted clear of the coast after all . . . ." There is, too, a rather too heavy reliance upon coincidence, even if we grant that in novels of this sort coincidence is one of the conventions of the game. On the other hand, the way in which the red-leather casket of jewels keeps appearing and reappearing throughout the story is an admirable adjunct to the plot: Roberts clearly knows the secret of suspense, which is to give us just enough information to chew upon but not enough to satisfy our appetite.

Another positive and admirable feature of the novel is its clever but never obtrusive use of Newfoundland dialect. Words such as "drook," "bully," "skinny-woppers," "spruce-tuck," and "up-along" give the reader the pleasure of novelty and the sense of being in a real but strange environment. And the use of dialect is only one admirable feature of the novel's style: whatever else Theodore Roberts could or could not do, he could write a lively, idiomatic, colorful but not over-decorated prose. His words are carefully chosen with a view both to their denotation and their connotations, and his sentences move forward with a lithe, easy grace.

Finally, I should like to pay tribute to the background of moral values which clearly but not distractingly lies behind the story. The novel obviously is a product of the courtly, courageous but strongly sympathetic gentleman whom I came to know in the last few years of his life. His code is not a particularly subtle or sophisticated one, but it is simple and strong: sympathy for the poor, tenderness towards women and all who are weak, courage in resisting the bully or the exploiter, patience in extremity. If such a code is out of fashion, so much the worse for the world of today.

Desmond Pacey

University of New Brunswick,
Fredericton, N.B.

1 ᵴᵴ *Black Dennis Nolan*

A T THE back of a deep cleft in the formidable cliffs, somewhere between Cape Race to the southward and St. John's to the northward, hides the little hamlet of Chance Along. As to its geographical position, this is sufficient. In the green sea in front of the cleft, and almost closing the mouth of it, lie a number of great boulders, as if the breech in the solid cliff had been made by some giant force that had broken and dragged forth the primeval rock, only to leave the refuse of its toil to lie forever in the edge of the tide, to fret the gnawing currents. At low tide a narrow strip of black shingle shows between the nearer of these titanic fragments and the face of the cliff. The force has been at work at other points of the coast as well. A mile or so to the north it has broken down and scattered seaward a great section of the cliff, scarring the water with a hundred jagged menaces to navigation, and leaving behind it a torn sea front and a wide, uneven beach. About three miles to the south of the little, hidden village it has wrought similar havoc, long forgotten years ago.

Along this coast, for many miles, treacherous currents race and shift continually, swinging in from the open sea, creeping along from the north, slanting in from the southeast and snarling up (but their snarling is hidden far below the surface) from the tide-vexed, storm-worn prow of old Cape Race. The pull and drift of many of these currents are felt far out from land, and they cannot be charted because of their shiftings, and their shiftings cannot be calculated with any degree of accuracy, because they seem to be without system or law. These are dangerous waters even now; and before the safeguard of a strong light on the cape, in the days when ships were helplessly dragged by the sea when there was no wind to drive them – in the days before a "lee-shore" had ceased to be an actual peril to become a picturesque phrase in nautical parlance – they constituted one of the most notorious disaster-zones of the North Atlantic.

We are told, as were our fathers before us, that one man's poison may be another man's meat, and that it is an ill wind indeed that does not blow an advantage to somebody. The fundamental truths of these ancient saws were fully realized by the people of Chance Along. Ships went down in battered fragments to their clashing sea-graves, which was bad, Heaven knows, for the crews and the owners – but ashore, stalwart and gratified folk who had noted the storms and the tides ate well and drank deep and went warmly clad, who might otherwise have felt the gnawing of hunger and the nip of the wind.

The people of Chance Along, with but a few exceptions, were Nolans, Lynches, Learys and Brennens. Their forebears had settled at the back of the cleft in the cliff a hundred years or more before the time of this history. They had been at the beginning, and still were, ignorant and primitive folk. Fishing in the treacherous sea beyond their sheltered retreat had been their occupation for several generations, brightened and diversified occasionally by a gathering of the fruits of storm. It was not until Black Dennis Nolan's time, however, that the community discovered that the offerings of the sea were sufficient – aye, more than sufficient – for their needs. This discovery might easily have been made by others than Black Dennis Nolan; but it required this man's daring ingenuity and powers of command to make it possible to profit by the discovery.

Black Dennis Nolan was but little more than a lad when he commenced the formidable task of converting a poverty-stricken community of cod-fishers into a band of daring, cunning, unscrupulous *wreckers*. He possessed a dominating character, even in those days, and his father had left him a small fore-and-aft schooner, a store well-stocked with hand-lines, provisions and gear, and a record chalked up on the inside of the door which showed, by signs and formulae unintelligible to the stranger, every man in the harbor to be in his debt for flour, tea, molasses, tobacco and several other necessities of life. So Black Dennis Nolan was in a position, from the very first, to force the other men of the place to conform to his plans and obey his orders – more or less.

For a time there were doubters and grumblers, old men who wagged their heads, and young men who sneered covertly or jeered openly; and later, as the rule of Dennis became absolute and somewhat tyrannical and the hand of Dennis heavy upon men of independent ways of thought, there were insurrections and mutinies. But Black Dennis Nolan was equal to every difficulty, even from the beginning. Doubters were convinced that he saw clearer than they, grumblers were satisfied, young men who jeered openly were beaten into submission with whatever weapon came most conveniently to hand. Dennis was big, agile, and absolutely fearless, and when he dealt a blow with an oar, a skiff's thwart, or a pole from a drying-stage, a second effort was seldom required against the same jeerer. Once or twice, of course, he had to hit many times and was compelled to accept some painful strokes in return. One or two of these encounters are worthy of treatment in detail, if only to show something of the natures of Black Dennis Nolan and his companions.

Immediately after his father's untimely death (the poor man was carried out to sea on a small pan of ice, while engaged in killing seals off the mouth of the harbor, in the spring of the year), Black Dennis was addressed by the title of "Skipper." The title and position became his, without question, along with his unfortunate father's schooner, store, and list of bad debts. The new skipper's first move towards realizing his dreams of affluence and power was to build a small hut of stones, poles, and sods both at the place of the broken cliff a mile to the north of Chance Along, and at the place of similar physical character three miles to the southward. It was winter at the time – a fine season for wrecks, but an uncomfortable season for spending one's nights in an ill-made hut, and one's days on the brink of a cliff, without companionship, gazing seaward through a heavy telescope for some vessel in distress. But the skipper had made his plans and did not care a snap of his finger for discomforts for himself or his friends. He knew that out of every ten wrecks that took place on the coast within twenty miles of Chance Along, not more than one profited the people of his harbor. They never went afield in search of the gifts of the treacherous sea. They took what they could clutch of what was thrown at their very doors, even then letting much escape them, owing to lack of science and organization. The new skipper meant to alter this condition of things – and he knew that the waters in the immediate vicinity of Chance Along were neither the most dangerous on the coast, nor the most convenient for the salving of wreckage and fast-drowning cargoes. So he established stations at Squid Beach to the northward, and at Nolan's Cove to the southward, and ordered Nick Leary and Foxey Jack Quinn to take up their abode in the new huts; Nick at Squid Beach, and Foxey Jack at the Cove, had to keep look-out for ships during bad weather and at night. Should either of them remark any signs of a vessel in distress he was to return to Chance Along at top speed, and report the same. Nick Leary and Foxey Jack Quinn were older men than the skipper by a few years, and the fathers of families – of half-starved families. Nick was a mild lad; but Foxey Jack had a temper as hot as his hair.

"What bes yer idee, skipper?" asked Nick.

Dennis explained it briefly, having outlined his plans several times before.

"An' how long does we have to stop away?" asked Nick.

"Five days. Yer watch'll be five days, an' then I'll be sendin' out two more lads," replied the skipper.

Foxey Jack Quinn stood, without a word, his vicious face twisted with a scowling sneer. Both men departed, one for the beach to the north and the other for the Cove to the south, each carrying a kettle and bag of provisions, a blanket and tarnished spy-glass. Black Dennis Nolan turned to other work connected with the great scheme of transferring the activities of Chance Along from the catching of fish to the catching of maimed and broken ships. He set some of the old men and women to splicing ropes, stronger and more active folk to drilling a hole in the face of the cliff, near to the top of it and just to the right of the entrance to the narrow harbor. Others, led by the skipper himself, set to work at drilling holes in several of the great rocks that lay in the green tide beyond the mouth of the harbor, their heavy crowns lifting only a yard or two above the surface of the twisting currents. All this was but the beginning of a task that would require weeks, perhaps months, of labor to complete. It was Black Dennis Nolan's intention to construct, by means of great iron rings, bolts and staples, chain-cables, hawsers and life-lines, a solid net by the help of which his people could extend their efforts at salving the valuables from a fast-breaking vessel to the outermost rock of that dangerous archipelago, even at the height of a storm – with luck. In the past, even in his own time, several ships bound from Northern Europe for Quebec had been driven and dragged from their course, shattered upon those rocks, sucked off into deep water, and lost forever, without having contributed so much as a bale of sail-cloth to the people of Chance Along. He was determined that cases of this kind should not happen in the future. The net was to be so arranged that the greater part of it could be removed, and the balance submerged, with but slight effort, and later all returned to its working condition as easily; for it would not be well to draw the attention of outsiders to the contrivance. Wrecking, in those days, meant more than the salvage of cargoes, perhaps. The skipper hoped, in time (should the experiment prove successful at the mouth of the harbor), to rig the dangerous and productive archipelago off Squid Beach and Nolan's Cove with similar contrivances. There was not another man in Chance Along capable of conceiving such ideas; but Dennis was ambitious (in his crude way), imaginative, daring, unscrupulous and full of resources and energy.

All day the skipper and his men worked strenuously, and at break of dawn on the morrow they returned to their toils. By noon a gigantic iron hook, forged by the skipper himself, with a shank as thick as a strong man's arm and fully four feet long, had been set firmly in the face of the cliff. The skipper and five or six of his men stood at the edge of the barren, above the cliff and the harbor, wiping the sweat from their faces. Snow lay in patches over the bleak and sodden barren, a raw wind beat in from the east, and a gray and white sea snarled below.

"Boys," said the young skipper, "I's able to see ahead to the day whin there'll be no want in Chance Along, but the want we pretends to fool the world wid. Aye, ye may take Dennis Nolan's word for it! We'll eat an' drink full, lads, an' sleep warm as any marchant i' St. John's."

"What damn foolery has ye all bin at now?" inquired a sneering voice.

All turned and beheld Foxey Jack Quinn standing near at hand, a leer on his wide mouth and in his pale eyes, and his nunney-bag on his shoulder. His skinnywoppers (high-legged moccasins of sealskin, hair-side inward) were glistening with moisture of melted snow, and his face was red from the rasp of raw wind. He looked as if he had slept in his clothes – which was, undoubtedly, the case. He glared straight at the skipper with a dancing flame of devilment in his eyes.

"What ye bin all a-doin' now for to make extry work for yerselves?" he asked.

There followed a brief silence, and then Black Dennis Nolan spoke quietly.

"Why bain't ye over to Squid Beach, standin' yer trick at lookout?" he inquired.

Foxey Jack's answer was a harsh, jeering laugh, and words to the effect that life was too short to spend five days of it lonely and starving with cold, in a hut not fit for a pig.

"Ye kin do what ye likes, yerself – ye an' them as be fools like yerself; but Jack Quinn bain't a-goin' to lend a hand a yer foolishness, Denny Nolan," he concluded.

"Turn round an' git back to yer post wid ye," said the skipper.

"Who be ye, an' what be ye, to give that word to me?"

"Ye knows who I be. Turn round an' git!"

"To hell wid ye! I turns round for no man!"

"Then ye'd best drop yer nunney-bag, ye foxey-headed fool, for I bes a-comin' at ye to larn ye who bes skipper here."

Quinn let his nunney-bag fall to the snow behind him – and in the same instant of time the skipper's right fist landed on his nose, knocking him backward over the bag, clear off his feet, and staining his red whiskers to a deeper and brighter red. But the big fellow came up to his feet again as nimbly as a cat. For a moment the two clinched and swayed in each other's straining arms, like drunken men. The awed spectators formed a line between the two and the edge of the cliff. Foxey Jack broke the hold, leaped back and struck a furious, but ill-judged blow which glanced off the other's jaw. Next instant he was down on the snow again, with one eye shut, but up again as quickly.

Again they clinched and swayed, breast to breast, knee to knee. Both were large men; but Foxey Jack was heavier, having come to his full weight. This time it was the skipper who tried to break the hold, realizing that his advantage lay in his fists, and Quinn's in the greater weight of body and greater strength of back and leg. So the skipper twisted and pulled; but Quinn held tight, and slowly but surely forced the younger man towards the edge of the cliff. Suddenly the skipper drew his head back and brought it forward and downward again, with all the force of his neck and shoulders, fair upon the bridge of his antagonist's nose. Quinn staggered and for a second his muscles relaxed; and in that second the skipper wrenched away from his grasp and knocked him senseless to the ground.

"Lay there, ye scum!" cried Black Dennis Nolan, breathing heavily, and wiping blood from his chin with the back of his hand. "Lay there an' be damned to ye, if ye t'ink ye kin say 'nay' when Dennis Nolan says 'aye.' If it didn't be for the childern ye bes father of, an' yer poor, dacent woman, I'd t'row ye over the cliff."

Foxey Jack Quinn was in no condition to reply to the skipper's address. In fact, he did not hear a word of it. Two of the men picked him up and carried him down a steep and twisting path to his cabin at the back of the harbor, above the green water and the gray drying-stages, and beneath the edge of the vast and empty barren. He opened one eye as they laid him on the bed in the one room of the cabin. He glared up at the two men and then around at his horrified wife and children.

"Folks," said he, "I'll be sure the death o' Black Dennis Nolan. Aye, so help me Saint Peter. I'll send 'im to hell, all suddent un' unready, for the black deed he done this day!"

That was the first time the skipper showed the weight of his fist. His followers were impressed by the exhibition. The work went steadily on among the rocks in front of Chance Along for ten days, and then came twenty-four hours of furious wind and driving snow out of the northwest. This was followed by a brief lull, a biting nip of frost that registered thirty degrees below zero, and then fog and wind out of the east. After the snowy gale, during the day of still, bitter cold, relief parties went to Squid Beach and Nolan's Cove and brought in the half-frozen watchers. For a day the lookout stations were deserted, the people finding it all they could do to keep from freezing in their sheltered cabins in Chance Along; but with the coming of the east wind and the fog, the huts of sods were again occupied.

The fog rolled in about an hour before noon; and shortly after midnight the man from Nolan's Cove groped his way along the edge of the cliff, down the twisty path to the cluster of cabins, and to Black Dennis Nolan's door. He pounded and kicked the door until the whole building trembled.

"What bes ye a-wantin' now?" bawled the skipper from within.

"I seed a blue flare an' heard a gun a-firing to the sou-east o' the cove," bawled the visitor, in reply.

The skipper opened the door.

"Come in, lad! Come in!" he cried.

He lit a candle and set to work swiftly pulling on his outer clothes and sea-boots.

"There bes rum an' a mug, Pat. Help yerself an' then rouse the men," he said. "Tell Nick Terry an' Bill Brennen to get the gear together. Step lively! Rouse 'em out!"

Pat Lynch slopped rum into a tin mug, gulped it greedily, and stumbled from the candle-light out again to the choking fog. He would have liked to remain inside long enough to swallow another drain and fill and light his pipe; but with Black Dennis Nolan roaring at him like a walrus, he had not ventured to delay. He groped his way from cabin to cabin, kicking on doors and bellowing the skipper's orders.

An hour and a half later, twenty men of Chance Along were clustered at the edge of the broken cliff overlooking the beach of Nolan's Cove and the rock-scarred sea beyond. But they could see nothing of beach or tide. The fog clung around them like black and sodden curtains. Here and there a lantern made an orange blur against the black. Some of the men held coils of rope with light grappling-irons spliced to the free ends. Others had home-made boat-hooks, the poles of which were fully ten feet long.

They heard the dull boom of a gun to seaward.

"She bes closer in!" exclaimed Pat Lynch. "Aye, closer in nor when I first heared her. She bain't so far to the south'ard, neither."

"Sure, then, the tide bes a-pullin' on her an' will drag her in, lads," remarked an old man, with a white beard that reached half-way down his breast.

"What d'ye make o' her, Barney Keen?" asked the skipper of the old man.

"Well, skipper, I'll tell 'e what I makes o' her. 'Twas afore yer day, lad – aye, as much as t'irty year ago – arter just sich weather as this, an' this time o' year, a grand big ship altogether went all abroad on these here rocks. Aye, skipper, a grand ship. Nought come ashore but a junk o' her hull an' a cask o' brandy, an' one o' her boats wid the name on all complete. The *Manchester City* she was, from Liverpool. We figgered as how she was heading for the gulf – for Quebec, like as not. So I makes it, skipper, as how this here vessel may be bound for Quebec, too."

Black Dennis Nolan took a lantern from another man, and led the way down the broken slope to the beach. The gear was passed down and piled at the edge of the tide. Dry wood – the fragments of ships long since broken on the outer rocks – was gathered from where it had been stranded high by many spring tides, and heaped on a wide, flat rock half-way up the slope. Another heap of splintered planks and wave-worn timbers was constructed on the level of the beach, close to the water – all this by the skipper's orders. The sea hammered and sobbed among the rocks, and splintered the new ice along the land-wash.

"If she comes ashore we'll be needin' more nor candle-light to work wid," remarked the skipper.

Again the dull boom of a gun drifted in through the fog.

"Aye, lads, she bes a-drawin' in to us," said old Barney Keen, with a note of intense satisfaction in his rusty voice.

THE BIG ship was hopelessly astray in the fog and in the grip of a black, unseen current that dragged at her keel and bulging beam, pulling her inexorably landward towards the hidden rocks. Her commander felt danger lurking in the fog, but was at a loss to know on which side to look for it, at what point to guard against it. He was a brave man and a master of seamanship in all the minute knacks and tricks of seamanship of that day; but this was only his third voyage between London and the St. Lawrence, and the previous trips had been made in clear weather. The gale had blown him many miles out of his course, and lost him his main-top-ga'ntsail yards and half of his mizzen-mast; the cold snap had weighted ship and rigging with ice, and now the fog and the uncharted deep-sea river had confused his reckoning utterly. But even so, he might have been able to work his vessel out of the danger-zone had any signal been made from the coast in reply to his guns and flares. Even if after the arrival of the men from Chance Along on the beach at Nolan's Cove, the heaps of driftwood had been fired, he might have had time to pull his ship around to the north, drag out of the current that was speeding towards the hidden rocks, and so win away to safety. There was wind enough for handling the ship, he knew all the tricks of cheating a lee-shore of its anticipated spoils, and the seas were not running dangerously high. But his guns and flares went unanswered. All around hung the black, blind curtains of the fog, cruelly silent, cruelly unbroken by any blink of flame.

Black Dennis Nolan and his men stood by the frozen landwash, along which the currents snarled, and rolling seas, freighted with splinters of black sea-ice, clattered and sloshed, waiting patiently for their harvest from the vast and treacherous fields beyond. A grim harvest! Grim fields to garner from, wherein he who sows peradventure shall not reap, and wherein Death is the farmer! Aye, and grim gleaners those who stand under the broken cliff of Nolan's Cove, waiting and listening in the dark!

A dull, crashing, grinding sound set the black fog vibrating. Then a brief clamor of panic-stricken voices rang in to the shore. Silence followed that – a silence that was suddenly broken by the thumping report of a cannon. The light flared dimly in the fog.

"Quiet, lads!" commanded the skipper. "Let the wood be till I gives ye the word. She bes fast on the rocks, but she bain't busted yet."

"An' she'll not bust inside a week, i' this sea," said one of the men. "Sure, skipper, the crew'll be comin' ashore i' their boats afore long. An' they have their muskets an' cutlasses wid them, ye kin lay to that. None but fools would come ashore on this coast, from a wreck, widout their weepons."

"Aye, an' they'll be carryin' their gold an' sich, too," said the skipper. "Lads, we'll do our best – an' that bain't fightin' an killing', i' this case, but the usin' o' our wits. Bill Brennen, tell off ten men an' take 'em along the path to the south'ard wid ye. Lay down i' the spruce-tuck alongside the path, about t'ree miles along, an' wait till these folks from the ship comes up to ye, wid four or five o' our own lads a-leadin' the way wid lanterns. They'll be totin' a power o' val'able gear along wid them, ye kin lay to that! Lep out onto 'em, widout a word, snatch the gear an' run fair south along the track, yellin' like hell. Then stow the noise all of a suddent, get clear o' the track an' work back to this Chance Along wid the gear. Don't bat any o' the ship's crew over the head if ye bain't forced to it. The gear bes the t'ing we wants, lads."

"Aye, skipper, aye – but will the sailormen be a-totin' their gear that a-way?" returned Bill.

"Sure, b'y, for I'll tell 'em as we bes from Nap Harbor, an' I'll send four lads to show 'em the way. After ye take their gear – as much as ye kin get quick and easy – they'll follow ye along the path to try to catch ye," replied Black Dennis Nolan.

Bill Brennen went up the twisty path to the barren, and along the edge of the cliff to the southward, followed by ten sturdy fellows armed with long clubs of birch-wood. Of the nine men remaining with the skipper, six were sent, along with the gear, to hide behind the boulders and clumps of bush on the steep slope. The skipper cautioned them to lie low and keep quiet.

"Ahoy, there!" bellowed the skipper.

"Ahoy! Can't you show a light?" came the reply, from the fog.

"Aye, aye, sir. Bes ye on the rocks?"

"Lord, yes! Show a light, man, for Heaven's sake, so we can get the boat away. Her back's broken and her bows stove in. She's breaking up quick."

The skipper and his three companions speedily made a small heap from the big pile of driftwood on the shingle, and lit it from the candle of a lantern. They poured a tin of seal-oil over the dry wreckage, and the red and yellow flames shot up. It was evident to the men on the land-wash that the unfortunate ship had escaped the outer menaces and won within a hundred yards of the shore before striking. She was burning oil now, in vast quantities, to judge by the red glare that cut and stained the fog to seaward.

"What sort of channel?" came the question.

"Full o' rocks, sir; but it bes safe enough wid caution," cried the skipper.

"Can't you show more light?"

"Aye, sir, there bes more wood."

A second fire was built still closer to the edge of the tide than the first.

"Stand by to receive a line," warned the masterful voice from the ship.

A rocket banged and a light line fell writhing across the beach.

"Haul her in and make fast the hawser."

Black Dennis Nolan and his three companions were most obliging. They pulled in the line until the wet hawser on the end of it appeared, and this they made fast to a rock on the beach as big as a house.

A small light appeared between the ship and the shore, blinking and vanishing low down on the pitching sea. The glare from the fires on the land-wash presently discovered this to be an oil-lantern in the bows of a boat. The boat, which contained about a dozen men, was being hand-hauled along the line that ran from the wreck to the shore. Black Dennis Nolan and his companions exchanged glances at sight of drawn cutlasses and several rifles and pistols in the hands of the men from the wreck. As the leading boat came within ten yards of the shore an officer stood up in her bows. By this time the light of a second boat was blinking and vanishing in her wake.

"Bear a hand to ease us off," commanded the person in the bows of the boat.

"Aye, sir, we bes ready to help ye," replied the skipper, humbly.

"How is the landing?"

"It bes clear, sir — shelvin' rock."

"How many are you, there?"

"We bes four poor fishermen, sir."

The boat rowed in and was kept from staving in her keel on the land-wash by Nolan and his men. The officer sprang from the bows to the icy shingle, slipped and recovered himself with an oath. He was a huge fellow. In one hand he carried an iron dispatch box, and in the other a heavy pistol.

"This lot of you?" he asked, glancing sharply at Black Dennis Nolan.

"Aye, sir, we bes only four poor fishermen," replied Nolan.

"I am glad to hear it. This coast has the name of being a bad place for shipwrecked people to come ashore on."

"You bes talkin' of the coast 'round to the south o' Cape Race, sir. We bes all poor, honest folk hereabouts, sir."

"Oh, aye," returned the other, drily.

By this time all the men were ashore and the boat was high up on the shingle, out of reach of the surf. The men stood close around it. They were well-armed, and kept a sharp look-out on all sides.

"What do you call this place?" asked the officer.

"Why, sir, Frenchman's Cove bes its name," replied the skipper.

Frenchman's Cove lies three miles to the south of Nolan's Cove; but the skipper was cautious.

"Do you live here?"

"No, sir. There bain't no houses here. We bes four poor men from 'way to the nor'ard, sir, a-huntin' deer on the barrens. We was makin' camp 'way back inland, sir, when we heard yer guns a-firin'."

"How far away is the nearest village?"

"Why, sir, this country bes strange to me, but I's t'inkin' Nap Harbor wouldn't be more'n ten mile to the south, fair along the coast. Bes I right, Pete?"

"Aye, skipper, I be t'inkin' the same. Nap Harbor lays to the south, maybe ten mile along, maybe less," replied Peter Nolan, a cousin of the skipper's.

A second boat reached the shore and discharged its freight of humans and small packages and bundles. This boat contained four sailors and ten passengers. There were three women among the passengers. All were clutching bundles of clothing or small bags containing their personal possessions of value. One of the women was weeping hysterically.

"Could we get a passage 'round to St. John's from Nap Harbor?" asked the officer.

"Aye, sir, I bes sayin' ye could. Sure there bes a fore-and-after i' Nap Harbor," said Nolan.

"Will you guide us to Nap Harbor?"

"Aye, sir, that we will, an' glad to be o' sarvice to ye."

"We will pay you well, my good man," said one of the passengers, a tall gentleman with a very white and frightened face, draped in a very wet cloak. "In the meantime," he continued, "let us dry ourselves at these fires and have something hot to drink. Where are those stewards, the lazy dogs!"

Two more boats came from the ship to the shore without accident. In the last to arrive were the captain and the doctor. The company gathered round the fires, keeping their boxes and bags close to them. The stewards and sailors brewed hot punches for all. The lady with the hysterics was soothed to quiet by the doctor and a tiny mug of brandy and boiling water. The officers held a consultation and decided to get the passengers safely to Nap Harbor, and aboard a schooner for St. John's and then to return to Frenchman's Cove themselves and salve what they could of the cargo of the ship, which was evidently of unusual value. (Black Dennis Nolan had expected this.) They would get help in Nap Harbor for the work of salvage, and would leave the four boats on the beach, under a guard of five seamen and the third officer. They had brought food from the ship, and so they ate a substantial meal while they warmed themselves and discussed their plans. But Captain McTavish neither ate nor drank, so bitterly did he feel the loss of his ship. He feared that even the moderate sea now running would break her up within forty-eight hours.

Black Dennis Nolan vanished in the darkness many times in the furtherance of his task of gathering wood for the fires. At last, after he had covertly inspected all the bags, bundles and dispatch boxes, he disappeared in the surrounding gloom and did not reappear at all. Dick Lynch, a man of about his own size, shape and coloring, – one of the six who had taken cover on the hillside – entered the firelight in his stead, carrying a fragment of broken spar. The change was not noticed by the men from the wreck.

Dry, warmly clothed, and inwardly fortified with food and drink, the ship's company set off for Nap Harbor, carrying as much as they could of their portable possessions, and led by four of the honest fishermen of Chance Along. They left behind them the third mate, a sturdy youth armed with two pistols and a fowling-piece, and five sailors armed with cutlasses and pistols – and enough dry and liquid provisions to last the guard for several days. They climbed the steep and twisty path that connected the beach with the edge of the barren, and soon their lanterns were lost in the fog. The third mate and his men brewed another generous supply of rum punch, heaped more wood on the fire and lit their pipes. By the time each had emptied his tin mug for the third time all felt inexpressibly sleepy. Mr. Darling, the commander of the guard, counted his men with a waving forefinger, and an expression of owlish gravity on his round face. Then, "Daniel Berry, you'll stand the first trick," said he. "Keep a sharp look-out and report anything unusual. Silas Nixon will relieve you at eight bells of the middle watch."

So Daniel Berry got unsteadily to his feet and stumbled away from the fire; but five minutes after his companions began to snore he returned to his blankets by the fire and fell fast asleep. He would never have been guilty of such a crime at sea; but ashore it was quite a different matter. What was the use of a look-out ashore? The island of Newfoundland was not likely to strike a reef or an iceberg. So he sank deep into the slumber of the just and the intoxicated.

A dawn wind, blowing gently out of the west, began to thin and lift the dripping fog. Out from the dark that hedged in the fire crawled six vague shapes which, as they came into the illuminated zone, proved to be Black Dennis Nolan and five of his men of Chance Along with ropes in their hands. They stooped over the blanket-swathed sleepers, working quickly and cunningly with the ropes. They also bandaged the eyes and mouths of the unconscious mariners with strips of blanket. By this time the light on the stranded ship was burning low. The skipper and his companions examined the four boats, dragged one of them down to the edge of the tide and launched it. The fog was thinning swiftly, and a gray pallor was spreading in the east and south. They manned the boat and pulled out for the wreck, following the dripping hawser.

The wreck lay across a sunken rock, listed heavily to port. Her spars were all over the side, a tangled mass washing and beating about in the seas. A snag of rock had been driven clean through the timbers of the port-bow. Black Dennis Nolan and his companions managed to get aboard at last. A fire of rags and oil still burned in an iron tub on the main deck. They went forward to the galley for a lamp, and with this entered the cabins aft. Dennis Nolan led the way. The captain's room was empty. They found and examined the quarters of the passengers. Clothing and bedding were tossed about in disorder, and it seemed that everything of value had been collected and carried away. They gathered up a couple of silk gowns and a fur-lined cloak, however. The skipper was shaking out the sheets from a berth when he felt something strike the toe of his boot. He stooped quickly, recovered a small box bound in red leather, and slipped it in his pocket. The others had observed nothing of this. In another cabin, they found the passengers' heavy baggage packed in about a dozen big leather boxes. They carried these to the main deck without waiting to open them. By this time the dawn was an actual, dreary-gray fact, and the fog was no more than a thin mist.

"Now for the cargo, lads," said the skipper.

They removed the tarpaulins from the main hatch, and broke it open. With the lamp in his left hand, the skipper descended into the hold by way of the stationary iron ladder.

"Pianeys," he shouted.

"Hell!" exclaimed the men on deck, in voices of disgust.

The skipper returned to the deck, after about ten minutes in the hold.

"The cargo bain't o' no use to us, lads," he said. "Pianeys, engines, an' fancy-goods."

They broke open the lazarette and found several cases of wines and brandy, and a quantity of provisions of superior quality. They lowered the passengers' baggage into the boat and pulled ashore through the spouting, slobbering rocks and reefs. In a second trip they salvaged the spirits and provisions. They carried boxes, cases and crates up to the barren, and hid them in a thicket of dense spruce-tuck, and concealed their gear of lines and boat-hooks in the same place.

"She'll last a good few days yet, if it don't blow up a gale," said the skipper, waving his hand towards the wreck, "and maybe we'll come back an' get some pickin's. But we bain't wantin' to raise any suspicions."

He loosened the bindings at Mr. Darling's wrists, so that they could be worked off in time, and then set out briskly for Chance Along with his three companions at his heels.

Of the future of the ship's company little need be said. On their way to Nap Harbor they were set upon and robbed by a large force of big men. Their valuables vanished into the fog and darkness, as if they had never been – and their guides vanished also. They went on, following the edge of the cliff, and reached Nap Harbor about two hours after dawn. From Nap Harbor they sailed northward to St. John's, and there reported the robbery to the police. The police calmed them with promises, and in time sent officers to Nap Harbor armed with search-warrants. Needless to say, the jewels and money were not found. Captain McTavish did not return to Nolan's Cove to salve the cargo of his ship, for the agent in St. John's explained to him that the task would be a profitless one. A few days later he was joined by Mr. Darling and the five men of the guard, and eventually they all sailed away. But the tall gentleman with the white face and the long cloak left a sting behind him. He was Sir Arthur Harwood, Baronet, and the lady who had wept hysterically, and been quieted by the ship's surgeon, was Lady Harwood. By the wreck these two had lost much of value in clothing, jewelry and money; but their greatest loss was that of a necklace of twelve flawless diamonds and fourteen rubies. Sir Arthur offered a reward of five hundred pounds for the recovery of this necklace. In this reward lay the sting.

In the little retiring harbor of Chance Along, Black Dennis Nolan was a great man. His plans had worked without a hitch – and still the carcass of the ship lay in Nolan's Cove, only waiting to be picked. A rich harvest had been gathered without the loss of a life, and without attracting a shadow of suspicion upon Chance Along. The skipper called together the twenty men who had shared with him the exertions and risks of that night. This was in his store, with the windows obscured by blankets, the door bolted and the lamp lit.

"Lads," said he, "here bes twelve hundred golden sovereigns. I makes 'em into twenty-four shares o' fifty each. Now, lads, step up an' each take a share."

The men obeyed, their eyes glowing and their hands trembling.

"Now there bes four shares still on the table," said the skipper.

"Aye, skipper, aye," stammered Bill Brennen, huskily. The others breathed heavily, shuffled their feet, gripped the money in their pockets and glared at the yellow pieces still glowing in the lamplight.

"FOUR SHARES still on the table," repeated the skipper. "Well, lads, one bes for Black Dennis Nolan."

He glared around at the circle of eager, watchful, shaggy faces set against the wall of gloom that hemmed in the table and the ill-trimmed lamp.

"Aye, skipper, that bes right," muttered Nick Leary.

"And another bes for the skipper who feeds ye all from his store."

Again he glared around, letting his dark, dauntless eyes dwell for a second on each face. "And t'other two bes for the lad who larned you how."

With that, he swept the four piles of coins into a pocket of his coat. One of the men grunted. The skipper turned his black but glowing regard upon him. Another cursed harshly and withdrew a step from the table. The skipper jumped to his feet.

"Who says nay?" he roared. "Who gives the lie to my word? I bes skipper here – aye, an' more nor skipper! Would ye have one gold guinea amongst the whole crew o' ye, but for me? Would ye have a bite o' food in yer bellies, but for me? An' now yer bellies bes full an' yer pockets bes full, an' ye stand there an' say nay to my aye!"

He pulled two pistols from beneath his coat, cocked them deliberately and stared insolently and inquiringly around.

"What d'ye say to it, Bill Brennen?" he asked.

Bill Brennen shuffled his big feet uneasily, and eyed the pistols askance.

"Thank ye kindly, skipper. Ye speaks the truth," said he.

"An' ye, Nick Leary?"

"Ye bes skipper here, sure – aye, and more nor skipper. But for ye we'd all be starved to death wid hunger an' cold," said Nick.

"An' what says the rest o' ye? Who denies me the right to four shares o' the money?"

"Me, Dennis Nolan!" said Dick Lynch. "I denies ye the right."

"Step up an' say it to my face," cried the skipper.

"Aye, step up an' give it to him straight," said one of the men. "Step up, Dick, I bes wid ye."

"Who said that?" roared the skipper.

"Sure, 'twas me said it," growled one, Dan Keen.

"Be there four o' ye denies me the right to the money in me pocket?" asked the skipper.

"Aye, there bes four o' us."

"Then step out, the four o' ye."

Dick Lynch, Dan Keen and two others shuffled to the front of the group. Black Dennis Nolan looked them over with fury in his eyes and a sneer on his lips. He called up Bill Brennen and Nick Leary, and gave a pistol to each of them, and exchanged a few guarded words with them.

"Dick Lynch, Dan Keen, Corny Quinn an' Pat Lynch, stand where ye be," he said. "Ease back along the wall, the rest o' ye. I'll larn ye who bes skipper an' master o' this harbor! I'll larn ye if I bes as good as the four o' ye or not."

He slipped off his coat, with the weight of coined gold in the pockets of it, stepped swiftly around the end of the table and sprang furiously upon the four men who had denied his right to four shares of the loot.

"I'll larn ye!" he roared.

Three of them, all husky fellows, stood their ground; but the fourth turned and dashed clear of the field of instruction. He was a small man, was Corney Quinn, and lacked the courage of his convictions.

The skipper struck the group of three with both feet off the ground. They staggered, clutched at him, aimed blows and curses at him. A terrible kick delivered by Dan Keen missed its intended object and brought Pat Lynch writhing to the floor, and before Dan fully realized his mistake something as hard as the side of a house struck him on the jaw and laid him across the victim of his error. Dick Lynch was more fortunate than his fellow-mutineers – for half a minute. He closed with the furious skipper and clung tightly to him, thus avoiding punishment for the moment. The two were well matched in height and weight; but the skipper was the stronger in both body and heart. Also, he seemed now to be possessed of the nerve-strength of a madman. He lifted his clinging antagonist clear of the floor, shook him and wrenched at him, and at last broke his hold and flung him against the wall. Dick landed on his feet, steadied himself for a moment and then dashed back to the encounter; but he was met by the skipper's fist – and that was the end of the fight.

Black Dennis Nolan returned to the table and sat down behind the smoky lamp. There was a red spot on his forehead from a chance blow, and the knuckles of both big hands were raw. He breathed heavily for a full minute, and glared around him in silence.

"Pick 'em up," he said, at last. "The lesson I larned 'em seems to lay cold on their bellies. Give 'em rum, Burky Nolan – ye'll find a case of bottles behind the stove. Drink up, all o' ye. T'row some water in their faces, too."

His orders were promptly obeyed. He took the pistols from Bill Brennen and Nick Leary, and laid them on the table, and then picked up his coat and put it on.

"Now, men, maybe ye know who bes master of this harbor," he said. "If any one o' ye, or any four o' ye, bain't sure, say the word an' I'll pull off me coat again an' show ye. Well now, we'll git back to business. The jewels bes still hid in the swamp. They bain't no manner o' use to us till we sells 'em. I'll do that, men, bit by bit, in St. John's. The grub an' liquor we took bes all in the pit under this floor. Ye kin come every day an' tote away what ye wants of it. The wines and brandy bes for them who has sick folks an' old folks to feed. Lift the trap, Bill, an' let them help theirselves."

Bill Brennen stooped and hoisted a trap-door in the middle of the floor. The skipper left the table, lamp in hand.

"Help yourselves, men," he invited. "Take whatever ye fancies."

They came up meekly. Even the three who had so lately been disabled obeyed the invitation, leaning upon their companions. The water and rum had revived them physically, but their spirits were thoroughly cowed. The skipper held the lamp over the square hole in the floor.

"Two at a time, men," he cautioned. "Bill, light a candle an' pass it down to 'em."

Half an hour later the store was empty, save for the skipper and the inanimate gear. The blankets had been removed from the windows, and the lamp extinguished. The skipper sat beside the deal table from which he had distributed the gold, staring thoughtfully at his raw knuckles. The pistols still lay on the table. He pushed them to one side, scooped the gold from his pockets, spread it out and counted it slowly and awkwardly. Then he produced a canvas bag, stowed the gold away in it and tied the mouth of it securely.

"A rough crew," he muttered. "They needs rough handlin', most o' the time, an' then a mite o' humorin' like ye t'row fish to a team o' dogs after ye lash the hair off 'em. Aye, a rough crew, an' no mistake – but Black Dennis Nolan bes their master!"

He left his chair, stepped across the floor, and lifted the trap that led to the cellar. He descended, returning in a minute with a bottle of wine and two tins of potted meat.

"I'm t'inkin' it bes about time to t'row some fish to that dog Jack Quinn," he murmured.

He went out, leaving the bag of gold on the table, and locked the door behind him. Though he left the gold he did not leave the pistols. Under his arm he carried the wine and the tinned meat. He went straight to Foxey Jack Quinn's cabin, and entered without knocking on the door. Quinn was sitting by the little stove with his head untidily bandaged. One pale, undamaged eye glared fiercely from the bandages. The woman was seated close to the only window, sewing, and the children were playing on the floor. All movement was arrested on the instant of the skipper's entrance. The children crouched motionless and the woman's needle stuck idle in the cloth. Quinn sat like an image of wood, showing life only in that one glaring, pale eye.

"How bes ye feelin' now, Jack?" asked the visitor.

The hulking fellow by the stove did not speak, but the hand that held his pipe twitched ever so slightly.

"Orders be orders," continued the skipper. "The lads who obeys me fills their pockets wid gold – an' them who don't get hurt. But I bain't a hard man, Jack Quinn. Ye did yer best to heave me over the edge o' the cliff – an' most would have killed ye for that. Here bes wine an' meat for ye an' the wife an' children."

He laid the bottle and tins on a stool near the woman. Quinn's glance did not waver, and not a word passed his swollen lips; but his wife snatched up one of the tins of meat.

"The saints be praised!" she cried. "We bes nigh starvin' to deat' wid hunger!"

"Twas me give it to ye, not the saints," said Black Dennis Nolan, "an' there bes more for ye where it come from."

He turned and went out of the cabin.

"I'll fix him yet," mumbled Foxey Jack Quinn.

The woman gave no heed to the remark, for she had already opened one of the tins of choice meat and was feeding the children from her fingers.

The skipper returned to the store, took up his bag of gold and went home. He lived with his grandmother, old Kate Nolan (commonly known in the harbour as Mother Nolan) and with his young brother Cormick. The cottage was the largest in the harbor — a grand house altogether. It contained three rooms, a loft, and a lean-to extension occupied by a pig and a dozen fowls. The skipper found the old woman squatted in a low chair beside the stove in the main room. This room served as kitchen, dining-room, general reception, and the skipper's bed-room. A ladder led up to the loft from one corner. Of the remaining rooms on the ground floor one was where the grandmother slept, and the other one was kept spotless, musty and airless for the occasional occupation of good Father McQueen, the missionary priest, who visited Chance Along three times a year. Cormick slept in the loft.

Mother Nolan glanced up from the red draft of the stove at her grandson's entrance. She held a short clay pipe in one wrinkled hand. She regarded the youth inscrutably with black, undimmed eyes, but did not speak. He closed the door, faced her and extended the heavy bag of coins.

"Granny, we bes rich this minute; but we'll be richer yet afore we finishes," he said. "This bag bes full o' gold, Granny — full o' coined English gold."

"Out o' the wrack?" she queried.

"Aye, it was in the ship, Granny."

The old woman puffed on her pipe for a few seconds.

"An' what else come out o' the wrack, Denny?"

"Diamonds an' rubies an' pearls, the wine ye drank last night an' the fancy grub ye et to-day. 'Twas a grand wrack altogether, Granny."

Mother Nolan wagged her gray head and returned her gaze to the red draft of the stove. " 'Twas grand wine," she muttered. "Wracker's wine! Dead man's wine!"

"Nay, Granny, there ye bes wrong. Not a lad aboard her was killed nor drownded."

"Then how come ye by the gold an' diamonds, Denny?"

The skipper laughed.

"Sure, Granny, I tricked 'em!" he exclaimed. "I made use o' my wits – an' the harbor bes rich."

"Saints pity ye, Denny! Rich? The folk o' this harbor bain't intended for riches. Take a care, Denny, for the devil bes in it. Saints presarve us! No good never did come to this harbor out o' wracks, Denny. Me own father was drunk wid rum out o' a wrack when he fell over the edge o' the cliff, an' broke his neck on the land-wash. It was for a case o' brandy out o' a wrack Pat Walen an' Micky Nolan fit wid skulpin'-knives till Pat was killed dead."

The skipper laughed again and expanded his chest.

"There bain't no fightin' over wracks now," he said. "I bes skipper now, Granny. Do this, do that, says I – an' it's done! An' I gives out the shares to the men like I was master o' a sealin'- ship after a trip to the ice – one share to every man o' the crew an' four to meself. There bain't no shares for ship an' owners in this business, Granny."

"An' where be the diamonds?" asked the old woman.

"Hid in the marsh, safe an' sound till I takes 'em to St. John's," replied the skipper.

"There bain't no luck in diamonds," mumbled the old woman, "an' there bain't no luck in wracks. The devil bes in the both o' them, Denny."

The skipper passed through his grandmother's bed-room and entered the cold and un-aired chamber that was reserved for the use of Father McQueen. He closed the door behind him, bolted it stealthily and then tiptoed across the floor to the bulging chimney and empty fire-place. He knelt on the drafty hearth, placed the bag of gold beside his knee, and thrust both arms into the black maw of the chimney. After a minute of prying and pulling he withdrew them, holding a square, smoke-smudged stone in his hands. Laying this on the hearth, he took up the canvas bag and thrust it into a cavity at the back of the chimney that had been ready for the reception of just such a treasure for some time. Then he replaced the stone and scrambled to his feet. He glanced furtively at the one small window which lighted the room, then moved noiselessly to the centre of the floor and put up his right hand to the whitewashed beam that crossed the low ceiling. His fingers searched delicately for a full minute; and then he lowered his hand, holding a small square of dry wood. The beam had been skilfully hollowed at this point. From the cavity he took a small box bound in red leather – the same small box that he had found among the sheets and blankets of a berth in the wreck. He opened it and gloated over a necklace of twelve diamonds and fourteen rubies glinting, flashing and glowing on a bed of white satin. He fondled the wonderful stones with his blunt finger-ends. So he stood for a long time, breathing heavily, his black eyes glowing like the rubies and glinting like the diamonds.

"A fortune," he murmured. "Aye, houses an' ships, liquor, food an' sarvants. Holy saint! I bes richer nor any marchant in St. John's!"

At last he closed the box, put it back in the cavity overhead, and returned the small square of wood to its place. He looked around the room. The fading light of the winter day was gray at the window. The curtained bed was a mass of gloom; a white Christ on a cross of ebony gleamed above the narrow chimney-shelf, between two candlesticks of dull brass; the floor, with its few rough mats, was as cold as the frozen snow outside. The skipper felt the chill of the place in his sturdy bones. He shot a glance at the crucifix. It, too, was an offering from the sea. His father had told him how it had come ashore in the hand of a dead woman, thirty years ago. Now the carven image of the Saviour seemed to gleam out from the black of the cross and the shadowy wall as if with an inner illumination. Black Dennis Nolan made the sign with an awkward and unaccustomed finger, and then went swiftly from the room.

The skipper, Bill Brennen and Nick Leary left their cabins stealthily about midnight, met on the snowy barren above the harbor, and tramped southward to the vicinity of Nolan's Cove. They worked for a little while in a clump of spruce-tuck, then moved off to another thicket about half a mile away, and there worked again.

"There bes some men in this harbor I wouldn't trust as far as I could t'row 'em over my back," said the skipper.

Bill and Nick agreed with him. The skipper glanced up at the starless sky.

"There'll be snow by sun-up," he said.

"Aye, skipper, a desperate flurry out o' the nor'-west," replied Brennen.

"D'ye mean wind, too?"

"Aye, skipper, mark that!"

All three felt a breath on their faces like the very essence of cold. They turned northward and set out on the homeward way.

All were snug in their beds long before the first pale hint of dawn. The icy draft from the northwest was a little stronger by that time, and it puffed a haze of dry and powdery snow before it. The night was full of faint, insistent voices. The roofs of the cabins snapped and creaked as if icy fingers were prying them apart. A sharp crackling sound came up from the harbor, where the tide fumbled at the edges of black ice. A dull, vast moaning that was scarcely a sound at all — something as vague, yet mighty as silence itself — drifted over the barrens and over the sheltered habitations out of the northwest.

When the skipper awoke in the morning the "flurry" was rolling over the brink of the barren, and down upon Chance Along in full force. The skipper piled dry wood — birch and splinters of wreckage — into the round stove, until it roared a miniature challenge to the ice-freighted wind outside. The bucket of water on the bench in the corner was frozen to half its depth. He cut at it with a knife used for skinning seals, and filled the tea-kettle with fragments of ice. His young brother Cormick came stiffly down the ladder from the loft, and stood close to the stove shivering.

"It bes desperate weather, Denny," said the lad. "Sure, I near froze in my blankets."

"Aye, Cormy, but we bes snug enough, wid no call to go outside the door," replied the skipper. "We has plenty o' wood an' plenty o' grub; an' we'll never lack the one or t'other so long as I bes skipper o' this harbor."

"Aye, Denny, we never et so well afore ye was skipper," returned Cormick, looking at his brother in frank admiration. "Grub — aye, an' gold too! I hears ye took a barrel o' money off that wrack, Denny."

"An' there'll be more wracks, Cormy, an' we'll take our pickin's from every one," said the skipper. "Times bes changed, lad. The day was when we took what the sea t'rowed up for us; but now we takes what we wants an' leaves what we don't want to the sea."

At that moment the voice of old Mother Nolan sounded fretfully from the next room.

"Denny! Cormy!" she called. "I bes fair perishin' to death in my bed. The wind bes blowin' an' yowlin' t'rough this room like the whole end o' the house was knocked out."

The skipper, who was as gentle with his old grandmother and as kind to his young brother as the best man in the world could have been, crossed the kitchen immediately and opened the door of the old woman's chamber. Mother Nolan was sitting up in her bed with a blanket on her thin, bent shoulders, and a red flannel night-cap on her gray head.

Her small face was pinched by cold and age, but her black eyes were alive and erect.

"The mats be squirmin' and flappin' on the floor like live fish," she exclaimed. "Saints presarve all poor creatures abroad this day on sea or land! They'll be starved to death wid the cold, Denny, for bain't I most blowed out o' my bed right in this grand house?"

The skipper realized that the room was colder than the middle apartment of the cabin had any right to be. He went to the window and examined it. The small frame was as tight in the wall as a dozen spikes and a liberal daubing of tar could make it. It had never been opened since the building of the house.

"The wind blows under Father McQueen's door like spray from the land-wash," said the old woman.

"'Twill be comin' down the chimbly," said Dennis, aware of the tide of icy wind low about his feet. He crossed the room and opened the door of the dismal chamber reserved for the use of the missionary. The sash of the window hung inward, the woodwork splintered and the spikes twisted, admitting a roaring current of wind and powdery snow. With a cry of consternation and rage the skipper sprang in, banged and bolted the door behind him, and went straight to the rafter across the middle of the ceiling. He removed the square of wood – and the hollow behind it was empty! For a moment he stood with his empty hand in the empty hiding-place, unable to move or think because of the terrific emotions which surged through him. At last he went over to the chimney and examined it. The bag of gold was in its place.

Now I MUST hark back a few hours to the time when the skipper and his lieutenants were on their way to the barrens behind Nolan's Cove to safeguard the interests of the harbor by changing the hiding-place of the common treasure of jewelry. They had not been gone half an hour from Chance Along before Foxey Jack Quinn slipped from his cabin and glided, like a darker shadow in the darkness, to the skipper's house. He was not ignorant of his enemy's departure southward. He knew that both young Cormick and old Mother Nolan were heavy sleepers; and, earlier in the evening, he had seen something through the window of the guest-chamber that had aroused his curiosity and a passion of avarice.

Foxey Jack Quinn was warmly clothed. His rackets and a light pack were on his back and his pockets were stuffed with food and a flask of rum. He was armed with a hatchet. He crouched beside the window of the empty room for several minutes, listening intently and fearfully. At last he wedged the strong blade of his hatchet between the sash of the window and the frame and prised inward, steadily and cautiously. With a shrill protest of frosted spikes the lower part of the sash gave by an inch or two. He devoted another minute to listening, then applied the hatchet to the left side of the window. He worked all round the sash in this way and at last pushed it inward with both hands until it hung below the sill by a couple of bent spikes. He thrust the hatchet in his belt and entered the room. He put up his hand to the rafter that crossed the low ceiling and so felt his way along to the middle of the room. Halting there, he removed the fur mitten from his right hand and felt about until his chilled fingers discovered a thin crack in the whitewash of the rafter. The little square of dry wood came away in his fingers. Next moment he held the leather-bound casket in his hand. He opened it and felt the cold jewels which he could not see. Then he closed it, slipped it into a pocket, replaced the square of wood in the beam and made his cautious way back to the window. He crawled over the sill, turned and tried to lift the sash upward and outward to its place. The sash came up easily enough but the bent spikes would not hold. After a few minutes of fruitless effort he turned away, leaving the window wide open. The sky was black as the throat of a chimney. A breath of wind came from the northwest. Foxey Jack Quinn was not weatherwise, however. He climbed the path to the edge of the barrens and turned to the north.

"Diamonds white an' red," he muttered. "I seen 'em, and I knowed what they was. Every little stone bes worth more nor all the fore-and-afters on the coast. I bes a rich man now – richer nor the governor, richer nor any marchant in St. John's – richer nor the king o' England, maybe. Holy saints be praised! Never agin will I wet a line at the fishin' nor feel the ache o' hunger in my belly. Denny Nolan will soon be cursin' the day he batted me about like a swile."

His plans for the immediate future were clear in his mind but for the more distant future they were vague, though rosy. He would make the ten miles to Brig Tickle in less than three hours, and from there turn a point or two westward from the coast and strike across country to the head of Witless Bay. He had a cousin in Witless Bay and could afford to rest in that cousin's house for a few hours. There he would hire a team of dogs and make the next stage in quick time. Dennis Nolan, who would not discover the theft of the diamonds until after sun-up, would be left hopelessly astern by that time. So Quinn figured it out. On reaching St. John's he would go to a shebeen that he knew, in a narrow and secluded back street, and there rent a room. Then he would commence the business of disposing of one of the diamonds. Just how he was to go about this he did not know, but he felt sure that Mother McKay, who kept the shebeen, would be able to give him some valuable advice on the subject. And after that? Well, the prospects were rosy but vague. He would get word to his wife in some way to move herself and the children to Witless Bay. He would send her twenty dollars, and after that, for the rest of his life, ten good dollars every month. As for himself, he would sail away to some big city "up-along" – to Boston, New York or London – dispose of the necklace stone by stone, buy a great house and live in idle luxury. He would dress like a merchant, eat hearty every day, drink deep and sleep warm. He had heard of such things – of men who never set their hands to a stroke of work from year's end to year's end. He would live like a king and drink like a lord and, like the good father and husband that he firmly believed himself to be, he would send ten dollars to his wife every month.

With such exalted dreams as these did Foxey Jack Quinn occupy his mind as he hurried northward along the edge of the snowy barrens. He had travelled about two miles when he suddenly became aware of the increased force and coldness of the wind. Snow as dry as desert-sand and as sharp as splintered ice blew against his face, stinging his eyes (one of which was still half closed), and smarting the battered flesh of brow and cheek. Then, for the first time, he realized that one of those dreaded storms out of the northwest was approaching. But for the treasure in his pocket he would have faced about and returned to Chance Along; but as it was he drew his fur cap lower about his ears, wound a woollen scarf around the lower part of his face and held doggedly on his way. The wind lulled for a little while, quieting his apprehensions. His rackets were on his feet now and he pushed along briskly over the pallid snow, through the whispering dark. He had covered another mile before the skirmishers of the storm rushed over him again out of the black northwest. That bitter wind soaked through his heavy garments like water and chilled him to the heart. Its breath of dry snow, embittered and intensified by its rushing journey across frozen seas and a thousand miles of frozen wilderness, blinded him, cut him and snatched at his lips as if it would pluck life itself from his lungs. He turned his back to it and crouched low, gasping curses and half-choked prayers to the saints. Then the full fury of the storm reached him, the dark grew pallid with flying snow-dust, and the frozen earth seemed to quake beneath his hands and knees. For a minute he lay flat, fighting for breath with his arms encircling his face. He knew that he must find shelter of some description immediately or else die terribly of suffocation and cold. Surely he could find a thicket of spruce-tuck near at hand? He staggered to his feet, stood hunched for a second to get the points of the compass clear in his mind, then plunged forward, fighting through the storm like a desperate swimmer breasting the surf. He thought he was moving straight inland where he would be sure to stumble soon against a sheltering thicket. But the onslaught of the storm had bewildered him. He struggled onward; but not toward the twisted clumps of spruces. His eyes were shut against the lashing of the snow and he held his arms locked before him across his mouth and nostrils. The wind eddied about him, thick as blown spray with its swirling sheets of ice particles. It struck him on all sides, lashing his face and tearing at his back whatever way he turned. ... A scream of horror rang out for an instant and was smothered by the roaring of the storm. So the spirit of Jack Quinn was whirled away on the tempest – God knows whither! – and the poor body came to rest on the frozen land-wash far below the edge of the blind, unheeding cliff.

The storm raged all day out of the northwest, and the folk of Chance Along kept to their cabins and clustered around their little stoves. Even Black Dennis Nolan did not venture farther than fifty yards from his own door. He replaced the window of Father McQueen's room, said nothing of his loss to Cormick and the old woman, and after breakfast went out and fought his way along to Foxey Quinn's cabin. He found the woman in tears.

"Where bes Jack?" he asked, drawing the door tight behind him and standing with his hand on the latch.

"He bain't here," said the woman. "He was gone from the bed when first I opened my eyes."

The skipper was a hard man in many ways, even then. Later, as he became established in his power, the hardness grew in him with the passing of every day. But always a tender spot could be found in his heart for women and children.

"He was to my house last night," he said. "He bust in a windy an' tried to rob me – aye, an' maybe he done it."

The woman covered her face with her rough, red hands and moaned like a wounded thing.

"I bain't holdin' it agin' ye," continued the skipper. "I fight wid men, not women an' childern. I fit Jack Quinn fair an' bate him fair. Let it be! If ye wants for food, Polly – whenever ye wants for food an' clothin' – send the word to me. I bes skipper in this harbor – aye, an' more nor skipper."

He turned then and let himself out into the shrieking storm. Polly Quinn stared at the door and the children clustered about her and pulled at her shabby skirts.

"Aye, he tells true," she murmured. "Never a hard word did Mother Nolan ever have from him. He was a good son to his mother an' the old skipper. But them as crosses him – the holy saints presarve 'em! Men-folks must be his dogs or his enemies. He batted me poor Jack nigh to death wid his big hands."

She turned at last and fed the glowing stove. Then she set about getting breakfast for herself and the children. There was enough hard bread in the house to last the day. There was a pinch of tea in the canister. Jack had drunk the wine from the wreck and taken away with him all that had been left of the tinned meats which the skipper had brought over the day before. The woman observed these things and gave some thoughts to them. She glanced up at the blinding white tumult against the drifted window, reflecting that her husband had taken the best food in the house – enough to last him for two days, at least – and had left behind him, for herself and three children, eight cakes of hard bread and a pinch of tea. Her faded eyes glowed and her lips hardened.

Black Dennis Nolan brooded all day by the stove with his big hands clasped idly between his knees. The grandmother sat near him, in a tattered armchair, smoking her pipe and mumbling wise saws and broken stories of the past.

"I bes a storm-child," she mumbled. "Aye, sure, wasn't I born a night in winter wid jist sich a flurry as this one howlin' over Chance Along – aye, an' wid a caul over me face. So I has the power o' seein' the fairies." And then, "me man were bigger nor ye, Denny. Skipper Tim, he were. Built the first fore-an'-after on this coast, he did." And later – "There bain't no luck in diamonds. The divil bes in 'em."

Young Cormick sat on the other side of the stove, busily carving a block of wood with a clasp-knife.

v ❦ *Father McQueen Visits His Flock*

AFTER THE storm from the northwest had blown itself out, a spell of soft weather set in along the coast. East and southeast winds brought fog and mild rains, the ice rotted along the land-wash and the snow dwindled from the barrens and left dripping hummocks and patches of black bog exposed. The wreck in Nolan's Cove had gone to pieces during the blizzard, sunk its cargo of pianos, manufactured cotton and hardware in six fathoms of water and flung a liberal proportion of its spars and timbers ashore.

Black Dennis Nolan felt as sure that Jack Quinn had perished in the storm as if he had seen him prone and stiff under the drifting snow. The fool had left the harbor that night, sometime before the onslaught of the blizzard, but after midnight to a certainty. He had gone out – and he had not returned! There could be no doubt about his miserable fate. The skipper pictured him in his clear mind as lying somewhere out on the barrens with the red-bound casket clutched in a frozen hand. So the skipper devoted a day to searching for him over the thawing, sodden wilderness behind the harbor. He took Bill Brennen and Nick Leary with him. The other men did not grumble at being left behind, perhaps because they were learning the unwisdom of grumbling against the skipper's orders, more likely because they did not care a dang if Foxey Jack Quinn was ever found or not, dead or alive. Quinn had not been popular. The skipper informed his two companions that the missing man had broken into his house and robbed him of an article of great value.

"We bes sure to find him somewheres handy," said Bill Brennen. "Foxey Jack was always a fool about the weather – didn't know east from west when the wind blowed. What was it he robbed from ye, skipper?"

"Whatever it was, ye'll both git yer share if we finds it," replied the skipper. "More nor that I bain't willin' to say."

He fixed Bill Brennen with a glance of his black eyes that made that worthy tremble from his scantily-haired scalp to the soles of his big, shuffling feet. Bill was one of those people who cannot get along without a master. In the past, for lack of another, he had made an exacting tyrant out of a very mild and loving wife; but since the masterful opening of the new skipper's reign he had snapped his fingers at his wife, who had ruled him for close upon twenty years. He was shrewd, though weak, and his heart was full of the stuff in which personal loyalty is bred and fostered. If the hand that beat him was the hand that fed him – the hand of his master – then the beating seemed an honorable and reasonable thing to him. True, the skipper had not yet lifted a fist to him; but in this case darkling glances served quite as well as blows. Bill had seen the strength of Dennis from the first and from the first had loved it as a thing to serve – as the spirit of mastery. Nick Leary, though a much younger man than Bill Brennen, possessed the same spirit of service.

The three searched the barrens all day, from sun-up to dark, north, south and inland. It was a gray day, sloppy underfoot and raw overhead. At one time the skipper halted and lit his pipe within three yards of the point of the edge of the cliff from which Quinn had pitched to his death; but wind, snow and thaw had obliterated all trace of those blindly staggering feet. The searchers explored the inner, tangled recesses of a dozen thickets of spruce-tuck, snarled coverts of alders, hollows hip-deep in sodden snow, and the pits and rocky shelters of knolls and hummocks.

"He bes hid away somewheres, sure's Saint Peter was a fisherman," said the skipper.

"Axin' yer pardon, skipper, I bes t'inkin' as how maybe he bain't dead," said Nick Leary, humbly. "Maybe he got t'rough to Brig Tickle, sir, an' from the Tickle he'd be headin' for Witless Bay this very minute."

The skipper shook his head.

"There bain't a man on the coast could live t'rough a flurry the like o' that widout he found shelter," he replied. "He bes dead somewheres widin t'ree or four mile o' Chance Along, ye kin lay to that, Nick."

They returned to the harbor after dark and said not a word to the others about the business that had occupied them throughout the day; Brennen and Nick Leary were asked many questions, but they lied valiantly, saying that they had been spying out boat-timber. Had they admitted that they had devoted a whole day to searching over the barren for the body of Foxey

Jack Quinn a suspicion that the missing man had carried away something of extraordinary value would have fired the harbor and set every able-bodied inhabitant on the quest. That would not have suited the skipper's plans. He did not want a knowledge of the necklace of diamonds and rubies to become general.

Doubtless the search for Jack Quinn would have been continued on the following day but for the unexpected arrival in Chance Along of the good Father McQueen. The missionary's visits were usually unexpected. He came now from the northward, on foot and unattended. In a haversack on his sturdy shoulders he carried food, two books of devotions and one of Irish poetry, and his vestments. Children who were playing a game called "deer-hunting" on the barrens behind the harbor were the first to know of the priest's approach. They shouted the news down to the gray cabins on the slope. A few of the men were working out among the rocks, under the skipper's supervision; others were cobbling skiffs and bullies that lay high and dry beneath the empty stages, and the old fellows were sitting around, giving advice and sucking at rank pipes. The harbor was at peace; and, what was still more unusual, it was free from hunger-fear. By the skipper's first important stroke of business his reign promised to be prosperous, even though tyrannical. At word that Father McQueen was sighted all work was stopped. The dories among the outer rocks were pulled to the land-wash. The men left their tarring and caulking under the drying-stages. Women issued from the cabins with shawls thrown hastily about their heads and shoulders. The skipper led the way up the twisty path to the level wilderness above. There was one man in the world whom he feared — feared without bitterness even as he did the saints on their thrones of gold. That man was Father McQueen.

Cap in hand, Black Dennis Nolan took the haversack from the priest and slung it on his own shoulder.

"Ye've walked a weary way, father," he said. "Ye bes mud and water to the knees, sir."

"But a step, Denny. Naught but a step, my son," replied the missionary, cheerfully. "I was in Witless Bay for two holy baptisms, a marriage an' a wake, an' I just took the notion to step over an' see ye all in Chance Along. *Pax vobiscum*, all of ye! My children, ye look grand an' hearty. How is Mother Nolan, the dear old body? Spry as ever, ye say? Praise the saints for that."

The people, men, women, and children, clustered round him with beaming faces, and in return he beamed at one and all, and spoke to a dozen by name. He leaned on the skipper's arm.

"But it bes still early in the forenoon, father," said Dennis. "Where did yer reverence sleep last night then?"

"Snug as a fox in his den, my son," replied the sturdy old man. "When dark came on I found me a dry cave in the side of a knoll, an' dry moss an' sticks for a fire."

"It bain't right for yer reverence to sleep out these rough winter nights," protested the skipper. "Maybe ye'll be gettin' yer death one o' these nights, sir."

"Nay, Denny, don't ye go worryin' about me," said the priest. "I am as tough as a husky."

He descended the path to the clustered cabins, still holding the skipper's arm and with the populace sliding and crowding at his muddy heels. His gray eyes were as keen as they were kindly. He remarked several of the great iron rings on the rocks to seaward.

"What are ye up to now, Denny?" he asked, halting for a moment, and pointing with a plump but strong and weather-beaten hand.

The skipper's black eyes followed the line indicated.

"That bes a grand idee o' mine, yer reverence," he answered, after a moment's hesitation. "Sure I'll tell ye all about it, sir, after ye get yerself dry alongside the stove."

"Something to do with wrecks, Denny?" queried the priest.

"Aye, yer reverence, it bes a part o' the gear for salvin' wrecks," returned Nolan.

At the skipper's door Father McQueen dismissed his followers with a blessing and a promise to see them all after dinner. Then, after a few kindly words to Mother Nolan, he entered his own room, where Cormick had a fire of drift-wood roaring in the chimney. He soon returned to the kitchen, in socks and moccasins of the skipper's, a rusty cassock and a red blanket. The innate dignity and virtue of the old man gave to his grotesque attire the seeming of robes of glory, in spite of the very human twinkle in his gray eyes and the shadow of a grin about the corners of his large mouth. He accepted a chair close to the stove – but not the most comfortable chair, which was Mother Nolan's. They knew his nature too well to offer him that. The skipper gave him a bowl of hot wine, mulled with sugar and spices, which he accepted without demur and sipped with relish. After a few minutes of general conversation, during which Mother Nolan expatiated on her rheumatics, he turned to the skipper, and laid a hand on that young giant's knee.

"So ye are preparing gear for the salving of wrecks, my son?" he queried.

"Aye, yer reverence, we bes fixin' chains an' lines among the rocks so as maybe we kin get a holt on whatever comes ashore," replied Nolan.

"A good idea," returned the other. And then, "Have ye had any wrecks already this winter?"

"Aye, yer reverence, there be'd one in Nolan's Cove."

"So? Did any of the poor souls come ashore alive?"

"Aye, yer reverence, every mother's son o' them. They come ashore in their boats, sir, an' left the ship acrost a rock wid a hole in her bows bigger nor this house."

"And where are they now?"

"That I couldn't tell, yer reverence. They set out for Nap Harbor, to the south, that very night, an' got there safe an' sound. An' I heard tell, sir, as how they sailed from Nap Harbor for St. John's in a fore-an'-after."

The priest regarded the skipper keenly.

"Safe and sound, ye say, Denny?"

"Aye, yer reverence, safe an' sound, wid their clothes on their backs an' food an' drink in their pockets an' their bellies."

"I am glad to hear it, Denny. Ye sent them on their way warmly clad and full-fed; but I'm thinking, my son, they must have left something behind them? It's grand wine this, Denny."

"Aye, father, it bes grand wine. It came out o' the wreck, sir, along wid a skiff-load o' fancy grub. There bes wine, spirits an' tinned stuff in every house o' the harbor, yer reverence. But the cargo weren't no manner o' use to us – an' the hull broke up an' went all abroad two days back."

"So ye got nought from the wreck but a skiff-full of drink and food?"

"I bain't sayin' that, father dear, though it were as peaceful an' dacent a wrack as ever yer reverence heard tell of. Maybe yer reverence bes buildin' another church somewheres? – or a mission-house? – or sendin' money up-along to the poor haythens?"

"Aye, Denny, I am doing all these things," replied the priest. "Since first I set foot on Newfoundland I have built nine little churches, twelve mission-houses and one hospital – aye, and sent a mint of money to the poor folk of other lands. My dear parents left me a fortune of three hundreds of English pounds a year, Denny; and every year I give two hundred and fifty pounds of that fortune to the work of the Holy Church and beg and take twice as much more from the rich to give the poor."

The skipper nodded. This information was not new to him.

"I was thinkin', yer reverence, as how some day ye'd maybe be buildin' us a little church here in Chance Along," he said.

"It would take money, my son – money and hard work," returned the priest.

"Aye, father dear, 'twould take money an' work. There bes fifty golden sovereigns I knows of for yer reverence."

"Clean money?"

"Aye, yer reverence."

"From the wreck, Denny?"

"Aye, father dear, from the last wrack."

"Without blood on it, my son?"

"Widout so much as a drop o' blood on it, so help me Saint Peter!"

"And the other lads, Denny? Are ye the only one in the harbor able to pay me something for the building of a church?"

There was the one question on the good priest's tongue and another in his clear eyes.

"I bes skipper, father dear, an' takes skipper's shares and pays skipper's shares," replied Nolan. "But for me there'd not bin one bottle o' wine come to us from the wrack an' the poor folks aboard her would never have got ashore in their boats for want of a light on the land-wash. As I kin spare ye fifty pounds for the holy work, yer reverence, there bes nineteen men o' this harbor kin each be sparin' ye ten."

Father McQueen nodded his gray head.

"Then we'll have the little church, Denny," he said. "Aye, lad, we'll have the little church shining out to sea from the cliffs above Chance Along."

Father McQueen was a good man and a good priest, and would as readily have given his last breath as his last crust of bread in the service of his Master; but for the past thirty years he had lived and worked in a land of rocks, fogs and want, among people who snatched a livelihood from the sea with benumbed fingers and wrists pitted deep with scars of salt-water boils. He had seen them risk their lives for food on the black rocks, the grinding ice and the treacherous tide; and now his heart felt with their hearts, his eyes saw with their eyes. Their bitter birthright was the harvest of the coastwise seas; and he now realized their real and ethical right to all that they might gather from the tide, be it cod, caplin, herrings or the timbers and freights of wrecked ships. He saw that a wreck, like a good run of fish, was a thing to profit by thankfully and give praise to the saints for; but he held that no gift of God was to be gathered in violence. In the early years of his work he had heard rumors and seen indications of things that had fired him with righteous fury and pity – rumors and hints of mariners struggling landward only to be killed like so many seals as they reached the hands to which they had looked for succor. The poor savages who had committed such crimes as this had at first failed to understand his fury and disgust; but with his tongue and his strong arms he had driven into their hearts the fear of Holy Church and of the Reverend Patrick McQueen. Even the wildest and dullest members of his far-scattered flock learned in time that life was sacred – even the life of a half-dead stranger awash in the surf. They even learned to refrain from stripping and breaking up a wrecked or grounded vessel that was still manned by a protesting crew; and with the fear of the good priest in their hearts (even though he was a hundred miles away), they would do their best to bring the unfortunate mariners safely ashore and then share the vessel with the hungry sea.

That even a deserted or unpeopled wreck should be common property may not seem right to some people; but it seemed right to Father McQueen – and surely he should know what was right and what was wrong! It was sometime about the date of this story that a missionary of another and perhaps less broad and human creed than Father McQueen's wrote to his bishop in the spring, "Thanks to God and two wrecks we got through the winter without starving."

Father McQueen did not hurry away from Chance Along. Six months had passed since his last visit and so he felt that this section of his flock demanded both time and attention. His way of knowing his people was by learning their outward as well as their inner lives, their physical and also their spiritual being. He was not slow to see and understand the skipper's ambitions and something of his methods. He read Black Dennis Nolan for a strong, active, masterful and relentless nature. He heard of Foxey Jack Quinn's departure and of the fight at the edge of the cliff that had preceded it. He heard also that Quinn had robbed the skipper before departing; but exactly what he had robbed him of he could not learn. He questioned Dennis himself and had a lesson in the art of evasion. He found it no great task to comfort the woman and children of the fugitive Jack. They were well fed and had the skipper's word that they should never lack food and clothing. He was not surprised to learn from the deserted wife that the man had been a bully at home as well as abroad. For his own part, he had never thought very highly of Foxey Jack Quinn. He visited every cabin in the harbor, and those that sheltered old and sick he visited many times. He was keenly interested in the work that the skipper was doing among the rocks in front of the harbor, and did not fail to point out persistently and authoritatively that chains and ropes designed to facilitate the saving of freights would also facilitate the saving of human lives. The skipper agreed with him respectfully.

On the morning of Father McQueen's arrival in Chance Along, the skipper dispatched Nick Leary to Witless Bay to learn whether or no Jack Quinn had reached that place. Leary returned on the evening of the following day with the expected information that nothing had been seen of the missing man in Witless Bay. In his pocket he brought a recent issue of St. John's newspaper, for which he had paid two shillings and two drams of rum. This he brought as an offering to the skipper – for the skipper could read print almost as well as a merchant and had a thirst for information of the outside world.

The first item of news which the skipper managed to spell out was the notice of a reward of five hundred pounds awaiting the person who should recover Lady Harwood's necklace of twelve diamonds and fourteen rubies and deliver it to Mr. Peter Wren, solicitor, Water Street, St. John's. The notice went on to say that this necklace, together with other smaller and less valuable articles of jewelry, had been taken by force from the shipwrecked company of the bark *Durham Castle*, which had gone ashore and to pieces in a desolate place called Frenchman's Cove, on the east coast. It also gave the date of the wreck and stated that if the necklace should be returned undamaged, no questions would be asked. The skipper saw in a moment that the reward was offered for the stones which he had found in the deserted berth and which Quinn had robbed him of. Five hundred pounds? He shook his head over that. He had read somewhere, at some time, about the value of diamonds, and he felt sure that the necklace was worth many times the money offered for its recovery. So the loss of it was known to the world? He had a great idea of the circulation of the St. John's *Herald*. He had retired to a secluded spot above the harbor to read the paper, and now he glanced furtively over his shoulder. No limb of the law was in sight. He gazed abroad over the sodden, gloomy barrens and reflected bitterly that the treasure lay there in some pit or hollow, in a dead man's pocket, perhaps within shouting-distance of where he stood. He swore that he would recover it yet – but not for the reward offered by Mr. Peter Wren in behalf of Lady Harwood. He re-read the notice slowly, following letter and word with muttering lips and tracing finger. Then, at a sudden thought of Father McQueen, he tore away that portion of the outer sheet which contained the notice.

The skipper returned to his house and found the missionary seated beside the stove chatting with Mother Nolan.

"Here bes a paper, yer reverence, Nick Leary fetched over from Witless Bay," he said. "It bes tored, sir; but maybe ye'll find some good readin' left in it."

The good father was charmed. He had not seen a newspaper for six weeks. He dragged a pair of spectacles from a pocket of his rusty cassock, set them upon his nose and hooked them over his ears, and read aloud every word save those which the skipper had torn away.

On the fourth night after his arrival Father McQueen drew a plan of the little church which he intended to build above the harbor.

"It will be the pride of the coast and a glory to Chance Along," he said. "Denny, I am proud of ye for the suggestion. Ye said ye'd give me a hundred pounds toward it, I think?"

"Fifty pound, yer reverence! Fifty pound bes what I offered ye, sir," returned the skipper, with dismay in his voice.

Father McQueen sighed and shook his head. A cold thrill of anxiety passed through Dennis Nolan. With the good father displeased there would be an end of his luck. He glanced at the priest and saw that he was still shaking his head.

The skipper loved his new store of gold because it meant the beginning of a fortune and therefore the extension of his power; but on the other hand he feared that to displease the missionary now in the matter of a part of that store might turn the saints themselves against him. And without the good-will of the saints how could he expect his share of luck? – his share of wrecks?

"I has seventy-five pound for yer reverence," he said. "It bes a powerful sight of money, father dear, but ye bes welcome to it."

"It is well, my son," returned the missionary.

The skipper felt a glow of relief. He had avoided the risk of displeasing the saints and at the same time had saved twenty-five pounds. Even when you earn your money after the skipper's method, twenty-five pounds looks like quite a considerable lump of money. He took up a candle and fetched the sum in yellow English sovereigns from his hiding-place.

Father McQueen devoted the following morning to collecting what he could from the other men of the harbor. The skipper had furnished him with a list of all who had shared in the golden harvest. It began to look as if the church would be a fine one. Not satisfied with this, he issued orders that the timber was to be cut and sawn without delay so that the building of the church should be commenced when he returned to Chance Along in June. He even drew up specifications of the lumber that would be required and the stone for the foundation. Then, leaving in the skipper's care all the gold which he had collected for the sacred edifice, he marched sturdily away toward the north. The skipper accompanied him and carried his knapsack, for ten miles of the way.

Two days after the missionary's departure a gale blew in from the southeast; and at the first gray of a roaring dawn the look-out from Squid Beach came hammering at the skipper's door with news of a ship on the rocks under the cliffs a few miles along the coast. Every man and boy who could swing a leg turned out. The gear was shouldered and the skipper led the way northward at a run, lantern in hand. They found the wreck about a mile north of Squid Beach, close against the face of the cliff. She had struck with her port-bow and was listed sharply landward. The seas beat so furiously upon her that every seventh comer washed her clean and sent the spray smoking over her splintered spars. She showed no sign of life. She lay in so desperate a place that even Black Dennis Nolan, with all his gear and wits, could do nothing but wait until the full fury of the gale should diminish.

It was close upon noon when the first line was made fast

between the cliff and the broken foremast of the wreck. The wind had slackened and the seas fallen in a marked degree by this time. Looking down from the cliff the men of Chance Along could see the slanted deck, cleared of all superstructures and bulwarks, the stumps of spars with only the foremast intact to the cross-trees and a tangle of rigging, yards, canvas and tackle awash against the face of the cliff. Something – a swathed figure, perhaps – was lashed in the fore-top.

The skipper was the first to venture a passage from the edge of the cliff to the foremast. He made it with several life-lines around his waist. He reached the bundle lashed to the cross-trees and, clinging with hands and feet, looked into the face of an unconscious but living woman. So he hung for a long half-minute, staring. Then, hoisting himself up to a more secure position, he pulled a flask of brandy from his pocket.

So Black Dennis Nolan brought back to consciousness the person who was to be the undoing of his great plans!

CLINGING TO the cross-trees, with the winter seas smoking over the slanted deck beneath him and the whole wrenched fabric of the ship quaking at every sloshing blow, Black Dennis Nolan pressed the mouth of the flask to the girl's colorless lips. A lurch of the hull sent the brandy streaming over her face; but in a second and better-timed attempt he succeeded in forcing a little of it between her teeth. He pulled the glove from her left hand – a glove of brown leather lined with gray fur and sodden with water – and rubbed the icy palm and wrist with the liquor. There were several rings on the fingers; but he scarcely noticed them. He thought of nothing but the girl herself. Never before had he seen or dreamed of such a face as hers, and a breathless desire possessed him to see her eyes unveiled. He worked feverishly, heedless of the yeasting seas beneath, of the wind that worried at him as if it would tear him from his leaping perch, of the wealth of cargo under the reeking deck and the men of Chance Along on the edge of the cliff. He returned the glove to the left hand with fumbling fingers, stripped the other hand and rubbed it with brandy. After finishing with this and regloving it he glanced again at the girl's face. The wet lashes stirred, the pale lids fluttered and blinked wide and two wonderful eyes gazed up at him. The eyes were clear yet with cross-lights at their depths, like the water of a still pool floored with sand and touched with the first level gleams of sunrise. They were sea-eyes – sea-gray, sea-blue, with a hint even of sea-green. Never before had the master of Chance Along seen or dreamed of such eyes.

The skipper was strangely and deeply stirred by the clear, inquiring regard of those eyes; but, despite his dreams and ambitions, he was an eminently practical young man. He extended the flask and held it to her lips with a trembling hand.

"Ye must swallow some more o' this," he·said. " 'Twill take the chill out o' ye."

The girl opened her lips obediently and swallowed a little of the spirits; but her crystal gaze did not waver from his face.

"Am I saved?" she asked, quietly.

"Aye, ye bes saved," answered the skipper, more than ever confused by the astonishing clearness and music of her voice and the fearless simplicity of her question. He scrambled to his feet, holding to the stump of the topmast with his right arm (for the spar whipped and sprang to the impact of every sea upon the hull), and looked at his men on the edge of the cliff. He saw that they were shouting to him, but the wind was in their teeth and so not a word of their bellowing reached him. By signals and roarings down the wind he got the order to them to bend a heavy line on to the shore end of one of the light lines attached to his waist. He dragged the hawser in with some difficulty, made it fast to the cross-trees, and then rigged a kind of running boatswain's chair from a section of the loose rigging. He made the end of one line fast just below the loop of the chair on the hawser. The second line was around his chest and the ends of both were in the hands of the men ashore. Without a word he cut the girl's lashings, lifted her in his arms and took his seat. He waved his left arm and the lads on the cliff put their backs into the pull.

The passage was a terrific experience though the distance between the cross-trees and the top of the cliff was not great. Neither the girl nor the skipper spoke a word. He held her tight and she hid her face against his shoulder. Fifteen of the men, under the orders of Bill Brennen, held the shore-end of the hawser. When the mast swung toward the cliff they took up the slack, thus saving the two from being dashed against the face of the rock, by rushing backward. When the mast whipped to sea-ward they advanced to the edge of the cliff. Five others hauled on each of the lines whenever the hawser was nearly taut, and paid out and pulled in with the slackening and tightening of the larger rope. But even so, the sling in which the skipper and the girl hung was tossed about desperately, now dropped toward the boiling rocks, now twirled like a leaf in the gale, and next moment jerked aloft and flung almost over the straining hawser. But the skipper had the courage of ten and the strength and endurance of two. He steadied and fended with his left hand and held the girl firmly against him with his right. She clung to him and did not whimper or struggle. A group of men, unhampered by any duty with the ropes, crouched and waited on the very edge of the cliff. At last they reached out and down, clutched the skipper and his burden, and with a mighty roar dragged them to safety.

Black Dennis Nolan staggered to his feet, still clasping the girl in his arms. He reeled away to where a clump of stunted spruces made a shelter against the gale and lowered her to the ground, still swathed in blankets.

"Start a fire, some o' ye," he commanded.

The men looked curiously at the young woman in the drenched blankets, then hastened to do the skipper's bidding. They found dry wood in the heart of the thicket and soon had a fire burning strongly.

"What of the others? Am I the – the only one?" asked the girl.

"Aye, ye bes the only one – so far as we kin see," replied the skipper. "There bain't no more lashed to the spars anyhow."

She stared at him for a moment, then crouched close to the fire, covered her face with her hands, and wept bitterly. The skipper groaned. The tears of Lady Harwood had not moved him in the least; but this girl's sobs brought a strangling pinch to his own throat. He told two lads to keep the fire burning, and then turned and walked away with lagging feet. Joining the men who were still tending the line that was attached to the wreck, he gazed down at the scene of tumult and pounding destruction without a word.

"The gale bes blowin' herself out, skipper," remarked Bill Brennen.

Nolan stared blankly for a moment, then aroused himself furiously from the strange spell that had enthralled his mind since first he had looked at the face of the girl lashed to the cross-trees. He swore violently, then flung himself full-length at the very edge of the cliff, and studied the position of the stranded vessel. He saw that she was firm on the rocks for almost half her length. She was badly ripped and stove, but her back was not broken. She seemed to be in no danger of slipping off into deep water, and as the wind and seas were moderating, she promised to hold together for several hours at least. He got to his feet and gave his opinion of the situation to the men as if it were a law.

"She bes hard an' fast," he said. "Wid the weather liftin', she'll not fall abroad yet awhile, nor she don't be in any risk o' slidin' astarn an' founderin'. We has plenty o' time to break out the cargo, men, after the sea quiets a bit. Aye, plenty o' time to sculp her. Now, I wants four o' ye to rig up a hammock o' some sort, wid lines an' a tarpaulin, an' help me tote the lady back-along to the harbor. Step lively, men!"

A few of the men ventured to show something of the amazement which they all felt by staring at him, round-eyed and open-mouthed; but he glared them down in short order. So four of them set about the construction of a hammock and the others crowded along the cliff and gazed down at the unfortunate ship. For awhile they gazed in silence; for wonder, and the fear of the skipper, were heavy upon them. What madness was this that had so suddenly come upon him? Had prosperity and power already turned his head? Or could it be that the young woman he had found on the wreck was a fairy of some kind, and had bewitched him with the glance of her sea-eyes? Or perhaps she was a mermaid? Or perhaps she was nothing but a human who had been born on an Easter Sunday – an Easter child. Strange and potent gifts of entrancing, and of looking into the future, are bestowed upon Easter children of the female sex by the fairies. Every one knows that! Whatever the girl might be, it was an astounding thing for Black Dennis Nolan to turn his back on a stranded and unlooted vessel to escort a stranger – aye, or even a friend – to shelter. They knew that, for all his overbearing and hard-fisted ways toward men, he was kind to women; but this matter seemed to them a thing of madness rather than of kindness; and never before had they known him to show any sign of infatuation. They glanced over their shoulders, and, seeing the skipper some distance off, supervising the construction of the hammock, they began to whisper and surmise.

"Did ye mark the glint in the eyes o' her, Pat?" inquired one of another. "Sure, lad, 'twas like what I once see before – an' may the holy saints presarve me from seein' it agin! 'Twas the day, ten year back come July, when I see the mermaid in Pike's Arm, down nort' on the *Labrador*, when I was hook-an'-linin' for Skipper McDoul o' Harbor Grace. She popped the beautiful head o' her out o' the sea widin reach o' a paddle o' me skiff an' shot a glimp at me out o' her two eyes that turned me heart to fire an' me soul to ice, an' come pretty nigh t'rowin' me into the bay."

"Aye," returned the other in a husky whisper. "Aye, ye bes talkin' now, Tim Leary. Sure, bain't that power o' the glimp o' the eye a mark o' the mermaid? They bewitches a man's heart, does mermaids, an' kills the eternal soul of him! Sure, b'y!

Didn't me own great-gran'father, who sailed foreign viyages out o' Witless Bay, clap his own two eyes on to one o' they desperate sea-critters one night he was standin' his trick at the wheel, one day nort' o' Barbados? Sure, b'y! He heared a whisper behind him, like a whisper o' music, and when he turned his head 'round there she was, nat'ral as any girl o' the harbor, a-gleamin' her beautiful, grand eyes at him in the moonshine. An' when he come ashore didn't he feel so desperate lonesome that he died o' too much rum inside the year, down on the land-wash wid his two feet in the sea?"

"Aye, Pat," returned Tim, "but I bain't sayin' as this one bes a mermaid. She was lashed to the cross-trees like any human."

"An' that would be a mermaid's trick," retorted the other. "Where be the other poor humans, then?"

At that moment the skipper approached.

"Mind the wrack, men," said he. "Make fast some more lines to her, if ye kin. I'll be back wid ye afore long."

The hammock was swung on a pole. Four men and the skipper accompanied the girl from the wreck, two carrying the hammock for the first half of the journey and the relay shouldering it for the second spell. The skipper walked alongside. The girl lay back among the blankets, which had been dried at the fire, silent and with her eyes closed for the most part. It was evident that her terrible experience had sapped both her physical and mental vitality. She had been lashed to the cross-trees of the foremast soon after the ship had struck the rocks, and fully eight hours before Black Dennis Nolan had released her. The second mate, who had carried her up and lashed her there, had been flung to his death by the whipping of the mast a moment after he had made the last loop fast about her blanketed form. She had been drenched and chilled by the flying spume and the spray that burst upward and outward from the foot of the cliff. The wind had snatched the breath from her lips, deafened her, blinded her, and driven the cold to her very bones. The swaying and leaping of the spar had at last jarred and wrenched her to a state of insensibility.

She spoke only three times during the journey.

"I would have died if I had been left there a little longer. You were brave to save me as you did. What is your name?"

"Aye, 'twas a terrible place for ye," replied the skipper. "I bes Dennis Nolan, skipper o' Chance Along; an' now I bes takin' ye to my granny, Mother Nolan, an' a grand, warm house. Ye'll have Father McQueen's own bed, for he bes away till June, an' a fire in the chimley all day."

Her only answer was to gaze at him with a look of calm, faint interest for a moment and then close her eyes. Ten minutes later she spoke again.

"The *Royal William* was bound for New York," she said. "There were ten passengers aboard her. My maid was with me – a Frenchwoman."

This was Greek to the skipper, and he mumbled an unintelligible answer. What could she mean by her maid? Her daughter? No, for she was scarcely more than a girl herself – and in any case, her daughter would not be a Frenchwoman. As they reached the broken edge of the barrens above Chance Along she spoke for the third time.

"In London I sang before the Queen," she said, this time without raising her pallid lips. Her lips scarcely moved. Her voice was low and faint, but clear as the chiming of a silver bell. "And now I go to my own city – to New York – to sing. They will listen now, for I am famous. You will be well paid for what you have done for me."

The skipper could make little enough of this talk of singing before the Queen; but he understood the mention of making payment for his services, and his bitter pride flared up. He gripped the edge of the hammock roughly.

"Would ye be payin' me for this?" he questioned. "Would ye, I say? Nay, not ye nor the Queen herself! I have money enough! I bes master o' this harbor!"

She opened her wonderful, clear, sea-eyes at that, full upon his flushed face, and he saw the clear cross-lights in their depths. She regarded him calmly, with a suggestion of mocking interest, until his own glance wavered and turned aside. He felt again the surging of his heart's blood – but now, across and through the surging, a chill as of fear. The flush of offended pride faded from his cheeks.

"Of course I shall pay you for saving my life," she said, coolly and conclusively.

The skipper was not accustomed to such treatment, even from a woman; but without a word by way of retort he steadied the hammock in its descent of the twisting path as if his very life depended upon the stranger's comfort. The women, children and very old men of the harbor – all who had not gone to the scene of the wreck save the bedridden – came out of the cabins, asked questions and stared in wonder at the lady in the hammock. The skipper answered a few of their questions and waved them out of the way. They fell back in staring groups. The skipper ran ahead of the litter to his own house and met Mother Nolan on the threshold.

"Here bes a poor young woman from a wrack, granny," he explained. "She bes nigh perished wid the cold an' wet. Ye'll give her yer bed, granny, till the fire bes started in Father McQueen's room."

"Saints save us, Denny!" exclaimed Mother Nolan. "First it bes diamonds wid ye, an' now it bes a young woman. Wracks will sure be the ruin o' ye yet, Denny Nolan! This way, b'ys, an' give me a sight o' the poor lamb. Lay her here an' take yer tarpaulin away wid ye. Holy saints fend us all, but she bes dead – an' a great lady at that!"

The stranger opened her eyes and looked at the old woman. Her wonderful eyes seemed to bewitch Mother Nolan, even as they had bewitched the skipper. The old dame stared, trembled and babbled. Turning to the gaping men, including Denny, she cried to them to get out where they belonged and shut the door after them. They obeyed, treading on each other's heels. Even the skipper departed, though reluctantly.

"May every hair o' yer head turn into a wax candle to light ye to glory," babbled the old woman, as she unwound the coarse blankets from about the girl's unresisting body. The other smiled faintly.

"I don't want to be lighted to glory – just now," she said. "I must sing in New York – to my own people – just as I sang before the Queen in London. But now I am so cold – and so tired."

Mother Nolan gaped at her.

"Glory be!" she whispered. "Eyes like fairies' eyes an' a voice like a mermaid's! An' the little white hands of her, soft as cream! An' the beautiful rings! Glory be!"

THE SKIPPER and his four companions returned to the cliff above the wreck, the skipper striding ahead, silent, deep in a mental and spiritual unrest that was thought without reflection. The others followed, whispering among themselves but afraid to question their leader. The wind had fallen to a breeze by the time they reached the point of the cliff overlooking the slanted deck of the stranded ship. Also, the seas had lost much of their height and violence, and the tide was ebbing. The group on the cliff's edge eyed the skipper inquiringly, furtively, as he joined them. He strode through them and looked down at the wreck. His face lightened in a flash and his dark eyes gleamed.

"What did I tell ye!" he cried. "Now she lays steady as a house, all ready to be gutted like a fish. Pass a couple o' lines this way, men. Take in the slack o' the hawser an' make her fast to yonder nub o' rock. Nick Leary, follow after me wid that block an' pulley. Bill, rig yer winch a couple o' yards this way an' stake her down. Keep ten men wid ye – an' the rest o' ye can follow me. But not too close, mind ye! Fetch yer axes along, an' every man o' ye a line."

Three minutes later, the skipper was sliding down the foremast, with Nick Leary close above him, another man already on the cross-trees and yet another in mid-air on the hawser. The skipper reached the slanted deck and slewed down into the starboard scuppers, snatched hold of a splintered fragment of the bulwarks in time to save himself from pitching overboard, steadied himself for a moment and then crawled aft. Leary, profiting by the skipper's experience in the scuppers, made a line fast to the butt of the foremast, clawed his way up the slant of the deck to port, scrambled aft until he was fairly in line with the stump of the mainmast, and then let himself slide until checked in his course by that battered section of spar. Taking a turn around it with his line, he again clawed to port, and scrambled aft again. His second slide to starboard brought him to the splintered companionway of the main cabin. Here he removed the end of the rope from his waist and made it fast, thus rigging a life-line from the butt of the foremast aft to the cabin for the use of those to follow. It had been a swift and considerate piece of work. The men on the cliff cheered. Nick waved his hand to the cliff, shouted a caution to the man at that moment descending the foremast, and then swung himself down into four feet of water and the outer cabin.

"Where be ye, skipper?" he bawled.

"This way, Nick. Fair aft," replied the skipper, "Keep to port or ye'll have to swim. I bes in the captain's berth; an' here bes his dispatch box, high an' dry in his bunk."

Nick made his way aft, through the length of the outer cabin as quickly as he could, with the water to his chin as he stooped forward in his efforts toward speed, entered an inner and smaller cabin by a narrow door and finally swam into the captain's own state-room. He grasped the edge of the berth in which the skipper crouched.

"Hell! I bes nigh perished entirely wid the cold, skipper!" he cried.

"Then swallow this," said the skipper, leaning down and tilting a bottle of brandy to the other's lips. "I found it right here in the bunk, half-empty; aye, an' two more like it, but wid nary a drop in 'em. There, Nick, that bes enough for ye."

Leary dragged himself up beside the skipper. As the deadlight had been closed over the port, the state-room was illumined only by a gray half-gloom from the cabin.

"This bunk bes nigh full o' junk," said Nolan. "The skipper o' this ship must ha' slept in the lower bunk an' kept his stores here. Here bes t'ree boxes wid the ship's gold an' papers, I take it; an' a medicine-chest, by the smell o' it; an' an entire case o' brandy, by Garge! Sure, Nick, it bes no wonder he got off his course! Take another suck at the bottle, Nick, an' then get overside wid ye an' pass out these boxes."

Nick was still deriving warmth from the bottle when a third man entered the state-room, with just his head and neck above water.

"She bes down by the starn desperate, skipper," he said. "Saints preserve me, I bes ice to the bones!"

At a word from the skipper, the last arrival took the bottle from Leary. Others reached the scene of action and the three iron boxes and the case of brandy were soon safe on deck. From there they were winched up to the top of the cliff.

"We'll break into the lazaret when the tide bes out," said the skipper. "She'll drain out, ye can lay to that, wid a hole in her as big as the roof o' a house."

They salvaged a few cases of tinned provisions from the steward's pantry. Five state-rooms were situated on either side of the main or outer cabins. They looted those to port first, where the water was only a few feet deep, finding little but clothing and bedding and one leather purse containing thirty pounds in gold. The skipper put the purse into a submerged pocket, and sent the other stuff to the deck, to be winched aloft. The cabins on the starboard side contained but little of value. A few leather boxes and bags were sent up unopened. The water was still shoulder-deep to starboard. The door of the fifth room on the starboard side was fastened. The skipper pulled and jerked at it, then lowered his head beneath the water, and saw that it was locked on the inside. But the lock was a light one, and the wood of the door was not heavy. He called for a capstan-bar; and in spite of the fact that he had to strike blindly under several feet of water, the lock was soon shattered. By this time, a dozen men were clustered around, their curiosity and greed uncooled by the cold water to their shoulders.

"There bes somethin' wort' salvin' in there, ye kin lay to that!" said one.

"The passengers' store-room, I bes a-t'inkin'," said another.

"Naught but the sail-locker," said a third. "D'ye look to find gold an' dimins in every blessed corner o' every blessed ship?"

At that moment the skipper pulled the narrow door open to its full extent. The water inside swirled out to fill the eddy made by the opening of the door; and then, slow, terrible, wide-eyed, floating breast-high in the flood, a woman drifted out of the narrow room into the midst of the expectant men. Death had not been able to hide the agony in her staring eyes, or dull the lines of horror in her waxen, contorted face. She floated out to them, swaying and bowing, one hand clutched and fixed in the torn bosom of her dress, a pendant of gold and pearl swinging from each ear.

A groan of wordless horror went up from the wreckers. For a moment they stared at the thing rocking and sidling in their midst, with grotesque motions of life and the face and hands of a terrific death; and then, as one man, they started to splash, beat and plunge their way to the companion-steps. The water was set swirling by their frantic efforts, in eddies and cross-currents which caught the dead woman and drew her, pitching and turning heavily, in the wakes of the leaders and elbow to elbow with some of the panic-stricken fellows in the second line of retreat. They knew the thing was not a ghost; they knew the thing was not alive, and could not harm them with its piti-ful, stiff fingers; they knew it for the body of a woman who had been drowned in her cabin – and yet the horror of it chilled them, maddened them, melted their courage and deadened their powers of reasoning. Even the skipper felt the blind terror of the encounter in every tingling nerve. The water was deep, the deck sloped beneath their feet, and the way to the flooded steps of the companionway seemed a mile long. The fellows who suffered the touch of those dead elbows that seemed to reach out to them beneath the churning water yelled wildly, lost their footing and power to advance at one and the same moment, and soused under, clutching blindly at their comrades. This brought others down and under who believed that the fingers gripping them were those of the poor corpse. Screams and yells filled the cabin and drifted up to the astounded men on the cliff. Heads vanished; legs and arms beat the imprisoned water to spume; fists and feet struck living flesh; and one poor, frantic fool clutched the unconscious cause of all this madness in his arms. Then the skipper, steadied from his first insanity of fear by the signs of disaster, lowered his head deliberately, plunged forward and downward, and swam under water for the companion. In his passage he wrenched floundering bodies aside and kicked and struck at floundering legs and arms. Coming to the surface and sinking his feet to the deck at the same moment, he grasped a step of the companionway and hauled himself out of the water, as if the devil were nipping at his heels. Turning on an upper step, he reached down, clutched two of the strug-gling fellows by the collars and dragged them up from the battling smother. One of them sprang on up the companion without so much as a glance at his rescuer, reached the deck with a yell, and started forward on the run without pausing to lay a hand on the life-line. His course was brief. The list of the deck carried him to the starboard. His foot caught in a splinter of shattered bulwark and he pitched overboard, head first and with terrific force, to the black rocks and surging seas. That was the last time Dan Cormick was seen alive – and the sight of him springing from the companion and plunging to his death struck horror and amazement to the souls of the men on the cliff.

Below, the skipper was doing his utmost to still the tumult

and drag the men to safety. They were the men of his harbor – a part of his equipment in life – and therefore he worked like a hero to save them from themselves and one another. His young brother was safe on the cliff; so his fine efforts were not inspired by any grander emotion than that felt by the shop-keeper who fights fire in the protection of his uninsured stock-in-trade. There were men below whom he needed, but none whom he loved even with the ordinary affection of man for humanity. The skipper yanked the men to the steps as fast as he could get hold of them, dragged them up to the level of the deck, and left them sprawled. All were breathless; some were cut and bruised; Nick Leary's left cheek had been laid open from eye to jaw in some way. The shouting and yelling were now over, and several husky fellows, ashamed of the recent panic, helped the skipper at his work. When the task of rescue was at last finished, the flooded cabin had given up three corpses be-sides that of the woman – four corpses and a dozen wounded men.

The bodies of the wreckers were hauled up to the top of the cliff, amid prayers, curses and groans of distress. The fellows on shore demanded to know who had killed them – and why? Knives were drawn. The brother of one of the dead men swore that he was ready and eager to cut the heart out of the murderer. The lads on the wreck caught something of all this; but it did not cool their desire to get ashore. Those who had the use of their limbs swarmed up the foremast and crossed over to the cliff. The first to step ashore was in grave danger for a half-minute; but he managed to throw some light on the thing that had taken place in the flooded cabin. Others landed, the whole story was told and knives were returned to their sheaths. The skipper, the seriously injured and the dead woman remained on the deck. The skipper was in a black mood. He knew his people well enough to see that this unfortunate affair would weaken his power among them. They would say that the saints were against his enterprises and ambitions; that his luck was gone; that he was a bungler and so not fit to give orders to full-grown men. He understood all this as if he could hear their grumbled words – nay, as well as if he could read the very hearts of them. He turned to Nick Leary. Nick had already bandaged his face with a piece of sail-cloth.

"Where bes the medicine-chest? Was it sent aloft?" asked the skipper.

"Nay, skipper, 'twas left below – in the captain's berth," replied Nick; his voice shook from pain and loss of blood.

"Ye bes cut desperate bad," said the skipper. "I'll go fetch the medicine-chest an' fix ye up wid plaster an' dacent bandages. Who says his leg bes broke? Ye, Bill Lynch? I'll fix yer leg, b'y, when I git the chest."

He looked up at the crowd on the cliff and roared to them to lower away some brandy for the wounded men.

"An' step lively, damn ye, or I'll be comin' up to ye wid a bat in me hand," he concluded, knowing that it was not the time to display any sign of weakness. Then he went down the companion, entered the water, which had drained out with the ebbing tide until it reached no higher than to his waist, and waded aft to the lost captain's berth. He felt decidedly uneasy, shot glances to right and left at the narrow doors of the state-rooms and experienced a sensation of creeping cold at the roots of his hair; but he forced himself onward. He soon regained the deck with the big medicine-chest in his arms. He was received by a growl of admiration from the little group of wounded. The men on the cliff looked down in silence, those who had taken part in the recent panic deeply impressed by the skipper's action. The brandy had already been lowered to the deck, and the bottles were uncorked. The skipper placed the chest on the upper side of the hatch, and saw to the fair distribution of the liquor. He passed it round with a generous hand; but the doses administered to Nick Leary and the man with the broken leg were the most liberal. He attended to Nick's cheek first, drawing the lips of the wound together with strips of adhesive plaster from the medicine-chest, and then padding and bandaging it securely with gauze and linen.

"That bes fine, skipper. Sure, it feels better now nor it did afore it was cut," mumbled Nick, gazing at the other with dog-homage in his eyes.

By this time, Bill Lynch, of the broken leg, was oblivious to the world, thanks to the depth and strength of his potations. The skipper cut away a section of the leg of his woollen trousers, prodded and pried at the injured limb with his strong fingers until the fracture was found, put a couple of strong splints in place, and bandaged them so that they were not likely to drop off, to say the least. He then made a sling of a blanket and sent his drunken patient swaying and twirling aloft in it to the top of the cliff. The other injured persons went ashore in the same way, one by one, like bales of sail-cloth. At last only the skipper and the dead woman were left on the wreck. The skipper stood with a scowl on his dark face and considered her. He drew the blanket sling toward him, and stood toward the poor clay.

"I'll send her up to ye for dacent burial," he shouted.

This suggestion was answered by a yell of protest from the men on the cliff.

"If ye be afeard o' her, ye white-livered swile, what d'ye want me to do wid her?"

"T'row her overboard! Heave her into the sea!" "Aye, t'row her overboard. She bes the devil hisself! T'ree good lads bes kilt dead by her already. T'row her overboard!"

"There bain't a man amongst ye wid the heart o' a white-coat," returned the skipper. "Afeared o' a poor drownded wench, be ye?"

This taunt was received in sullen silence. The skipper stood firm on the listed deck, his feet set well apart and his shoulders squared, and leered up at them. Then, stooping forward quickly, he plucked the pendants from those bloodless ears, and set the body rolling into the starboard scuppers and overboard to the frothing surf and slobbering rocks. From the cliff a cry as of mingled relief and dismay rang down to him. He moved forward and swarmed the foremast to the cross-trees. There he paused for a few moments to glance across. He saw that Bill Brennen, Nick Leary, his brother Cormick and several of the men whom he had rescued from the flooded cabin had clustered around the shore-end of the hawser. He saw that they feared treachery. He made his way across, cool, fearless, with a dangerous smile on his lips.

"SHE LAYS snug enough. We'll break out the freight, to-morrow," said the skipper.

"Aye, skipper, aye," returned Bill Brennen, with an unsuccessful attempt to put some heartiness into his tones; but the others did not say a word. They made litters for the dead and wounded, gathered up the spoils of the cabins, and set off sullenly for Chance Along. The skipper stood to one side and watched them from under lowering brows. At the first stroke of misfortune they were sulking and snarling at him like a pack of wolf-dogs. They evidently expected a boat-load of gold from every wreck, and no casualties. He despised and hated them. He hurried after them and called a halt. He ordered them to break open the ship's boxes. They obeyed him in sullen wonder.

"If ye find any gold," he said, "count it an' divide it amongst ye. An' the same wid the rest o' the gear. An' here bes somethin' more for ye!" He tossed the purse and the earrings to them. "Take 'em. Keep 'em. I take no shares wid a crew like ye – not this time, anyhow, ye cowardly, unthankful, treacherous swabs! Aye, count the gold, damn ye! an' stow it away in yer pockets. I bes makin' rich men o' ye – an' at a turn o' bad luck ye all be ready to knife me. D'ye think I kilt them t'ree dead fools? Nay, they kilt themselves wid fear of a poor drownded woman! T'ree more would ha' bin stunned an' drownded but for me. Holy saints above! I bes minded to leave ye to fish an' starve – all o' ye save them as has stood to me like men an' them o' me own blood – an' go to another harbor. Ye white-livered pack o' wolf-breed huskies! Ye cowardly, snarlin', treacherous divils. Take yer money. I gives it to ye. Go home an' feed on the good grub I gives to ye an' drink the liquor ye'd never have the wits nor the courage to salve but for me! Go home wid ye, out o' my sight, or maybe I'll forgit the flabby-hearted swabs ye be an' give ye a taste o' me bat!"

The skipper's fury increased with the utterance of every bellowed word. His dark face burned crimson, and his black eyes glowed like coals in the open draught of a stove. His teeth flashed between his snarling lips like a timber-wolf's fangs. He shook his fist at them, picked up a birch billet, which was a part of the wrecking-gear, and swung it threateningly. About eight of the men and boys, including young Cormick Nolan, Nick Leary and Bill Brennen, stood away from the others, out of line of the skipper's frantic gestures and bruising words. Some of them were loyal, some simply more afraid of Black Dennis Nolan than of anything else in the world. But fear, after all, is an important element in a certain quality of devotion.

The main party were somewhat shaken. A few of them growled back at the skipper; but not quite loud enough to claim his attention to them in particular. Some eyed him apprehensively, while others broke open the ship's and passengers' boxes. They found minted money only in one of the captain's dispatch-boxes – two small but weighty bags of gold containing about two hundred sovereigns in all. This was the money which the dead captain had been armed with by his owners against harbor-dues, etc. The funds which the passengers must have possessed had doubtless been flung overboard and under along with the unfortunate beings who had clung to them. The sullen, greedy fellows began to count and divide the gold. They were slow, suspicious, grasping. The skipper, having fallen to a glowing silence at last, watched them for a minute or two with a bitter sneer on his face. Then he turned and set out briskly for Chance Along. The loyal and fearful party followed him, most of them with evident reluctance. A few turned their faces continually to gaze at the distributing of the gold and gear. The skipper noted this with a sidelong, covert glance.

"Don't ye be worryin', men. Ye'll have yer fill afore long, so help me Saint Peter!" he exclaimed. "No man who stands by me, an' knows me for master, goes empty!"

He did not speak another word on the way or so much as look at his followers. He strode along swiftly, thinking hard. He could not blink the fact that the needless deaths of the three men in the cabin of the *Royal William* had weakened his position seriously. He could not blink the ugly fact that the day's activities had bred a mutiny – and that the mutiny had not yet been faced and broken. It was still breeding. The poison was still working. In a fit of blind anger and unreasoning disgust he had fed the spirit of rebellion with gold. He had shattered with his boot what he had built with his hands. The work of mastery was all to do over again. He had taught them that his rights were four shares to one – and now he had given them all, thereby destroying a precedent in the establishing of which he had risked his life and robbing himself and his loyal followers at the same time. The situation was desperate; but he could not find it in his heart to regret the day's work; for there was the girl with the sea-eyes, lying safe in his own house this very minute! A thrill, sweet yet bitter, went through his blood at the thought. No other woman had ever caused him a choking pang like this. The remembrance of those clear eyes shook him to the very soul and quenched his burning anger with a wave of strangely mingled adoration and desire. He was little more than a fine animal, after all. The man in him lay passive and un-developed under the tides of passion, craving, brute-pride and crude ambitions. But the manhood was there, as his flawless courage and unconsidered kindness to women and children indicated. But he was self-centred, violent, brutally masterful. Women and children had always seemed to him (until now) help-less, harmless things, that had a right to the protection of men even as they had a right to remain ashore from the danger of wind and sea. The stag caribou and the dog-wolf have the same attitude toward the females of their races. It is a characteristic which is natural to animals and boasted of by civilized men. Dogs and gentlemen do not bite and beat their females; and if Black Dennis Nolan resembled a stag, a he-wolf, and a dog in many points, in this particular he also resembled a gentleman. Like some hammering old feudal baron of the Norman time and the finer type, his battles were all with men. Those who did not ride behind him he rode against. He feared the saints and a priest, even as did the barons of old; but all others must acknow-ledge his lordship or know themselves for his enemies. To Black Dennis Nolan the law of the land was a vague thing not greatly respected. To Walter, Lord of Waltham, William the Red was a vague personage, not greatly respected. Walter, Lord of Waltham, son of Walter and grandson of Fitz Oof of Nor-mandy; Skipper of Chance Along, son of Skipper Pat and grand-son of Skipper Tim – the two barons differed only in period and location. In short, Black Dennis Nolan possessed many of the qualities of strong animals, of a feudal baron, and one at least of a modern gentleman.

The skipper was overtaken and joined by his young brother at the edge of the barrens above Chance Along. They scrambled swiftly down the path to the clustered cabins. At their own door Cormick plucked the skipper's sleeve.

"They was talkin' o' witches," he whispered. "Dick Lynch an' some more o' the lads. They says as how the comather was put on to ye this very mornin', Denny."

The skipper paused with his hand on the latch and eyed the other sharply.

"Witches, ye say? An' Dick Lynch was talkin', was he? Who did they figger as put the spell on to me?"

"The lass ye saved from the fore-top. Sure, that's what they all bes sayin', Denny. Mermaid, they calls her – an' some a fairy. A witch, anyhow. They says as how yer luck bes turned now – aye, the luck o' the entire harbor. 'Twas herself – the spell o' her – kilt the t'ree lads in the cabin, they be sayin'. Their talk was desperate black, Denny."

"'Twas the poor dead, drownded woman, an' their own cowardly souls, kilt 'em!"

"Aye, Denny, so it was, nary a doubt; but they shot ye some desperate black looks, Denny."

"Well, Cormy, don't ye be worryin'. Fifty t'ousand squid like Dick Lynch couldn't frighten me. The comather, ye say? Saints o' God! but I'll be puttin' it on themselves wid a club! Bewitched? What the divil do they know o' witches? Fishes bes all they understands! Black looks they give me, did they? I'll be batin' 'em so black they'll all look like rotted herrings, by the Holy Peter hisself! Aye, Cormy, don't ye worry, now."

At that he opened the door quietly and stepped inside with a strange air of reverence and eagerness. The boy followed softly and closed the door behind him. The fire roared and crackled in the round stove, but the room was empty of human life. Wet garments of fine linen hung on a line behind the stove. The inner door opened and old Mother Nolan hobbled into the kitchen with a wrinkled finger to her lips.

"Whist wid ye!" she cautioned. "She be sleepin' like a babe, the poor darlint, in Father McQueen's own bed, wid everything snug an' warm as ye'd find in any marchant's grand house in St. John's."

She took her accustomed seat beside the stove and lit her pipe.

"Saints alive! but can't ye set down!" she exclaimed. "I wants to talk wid ye, b'ys. Tell me this – where bes t'e rest o' the poor folk from the wrack?"

"She bes the only livin' soul we found, Granny," replied the skipper. "She was lashed in the foremast – an' t'other spars was all over the side. We found a poor dead body in one o' the cabins – drownded to death – an' not so much as another corpse. Aye, Granny, 'twas a desperate cruel wrack altogether."

The old woman shot a keen glance at him; but he returned it without a blink.

"Didn't ye find no more gold an' diamonds, then?" she asked.

"We found some gold. I give it all to the men."

"An' what was the cargo?"

"Sure, Granny, we didn't break into her cargo yet. There was a rumpus – aye, ye may well call it a rumpus! Did ye say as she bes sleepin', Granny?"

The old woman nodded her head, her black eyes fixed on the red draught of the stove with a faraway, fateful, veiled glint in them which her grandsons knew well. She had ceased to puff at her pipe for the moment, and in the failing light from the window they could see a thin reek of smoke trailing straight up from the bowl.

"Aye, sleepin'," she mumbled, at last. "Saints presarve us, Denny! There bes fairy blood in her – aye, fairy blood. Sure, can't ye see it in her eyes? I's afeard there bain't no luck in it, Denny. Worse nor wracked diamonds, worse nor wracked gold they be – these humans wid fairy blood in 'em! And don't I know? Sure, wasn't me own grandmother own cousin to the darter o' a fairy-woman? Sure she was, back in Old Tyoon. An' there was no luck in the house wid her; an' she was a beauty, too, like the darlint body yonder."

The skipper smiled and lit his pipe. The winter twilight had deepened to gloom. The front of the stove glowed like a long, half-closed red eye, and young Cormick peered fearfully at the black corners of the room. The skipper left his chair, fetched a candle from the dresser and lit it at the door of the stove.

"We bes a long way off from old Tyoon, Granny," he said; "an' maybe there bain't no fairies now, even in Tyoon. I never seen no fairy in Chance Along, anyhow; nor witch, mermaid, pixie, bogey, ghost, sprite – no, nor even a corpus-light. Herself in yonder bes no fairy-child, Granny, but a fine young lady, more beautiful nor an angel in heaven – maybe a marchant's darter an' maybe a king's darter, but nary the child o' any vanishin' sprite. Sure, didn't I hold her in me two arms all the way from the foretop o' the wrack to the cliff? – an' didn't she weigh agin' me arms till they was nigh broke wid it?"

"Denny, ye poor fool," returned Mother Nolan, "ye bes

simple as a squid t'rowed up on the land-wash. What do ye know o' fairies an' the like? Wasn't I born on a Easter Sunday, wid the power to see the good people, an' the little people, an' all the tricksy tribes? The body o' a fairy-child bes human, lad. 'Tis but the heart o' her bes unhuman – an' the beauty o' her – an' there bain't no soul in her. Did ye hear the voice o' her, Denny? Holy saints! But was there ever a human woman wid a voice the like o' that?"

"Aye, Granny, but did she eat? Did she drink? Did she shed tears?" asked the skipper.

The old woman nodded her head.

"Fairies don't shed tears," said Dennis, grinning. "Sure, ye've told me that yerself many a time."

"But half-fairies, like herself, sheds 'em as well as any human, ye mad fool," returned Mother Nolan.

At that moment the outer door opened, and Nick Leary entered the kitchen, closing the door behind him, and shooting the bolt into its place. His face was so generously bandaged that only his eyes and nose were visible. He glanced fearfully around the room.

"Where bes the mermaid? Has she flew away?" he whispered.

The skipper sprang to his feet with an oath.

"Mermaid?" he cried. "Ye dodderin' fool ye? She bes no more a mermaid nor any fat wench in Chance Along! Has she flew, ye say! How to hell kin a mermaid fly? Wid her tail? Ye bes a true man, Nick, or I'd bat ye over the nob for yer trouble. She bes a poor young woman saved from a wrack, as well ye know. What d'ye want wid me?"

Leary trembled, big as he was, and pulled off his fur cap with both hands.

"Aye, skipper, aye! but where bes she now?" he whispered.

"She bes sleepin' like any poor babe in his reverence's own bed," replied the skipper.

"Saints presarve us!" exclaimed the other. "In the blessed father's bed! I bain't sayin' naught, skipper, sir, but – but sure 'twill be desperate bad luck for his reverence!"

Black Dennis Nolan lost his temper then. He gripped Nick by the shoulder, swore at him, shook him about, and threatened to knock his head off. Had Nick been one of the mutineers, the chances are ten to one that he would have been floored and beaten half to death. But even in the full fury of his rage the skipper did not lose sight of the fact that this fellow was a loyal slave. He did not love Nick, but he loved his dog-like devotion. So he kept his right hand down at his side, and it cost him a mighty effort of restraint, and contented himself with cursing and shaking. The boy stared at the two wide-eyed, and the old woman smoked and nodded without so much as a glance at them. At last the skipper unhooked his fingers from Nick's shoulder, laughed harshly and returned to his seat.

"Luck?" he said, derisively. "The luck o' Father McQueen bes the protection o' the holy saints above. An' my luck bes the strength o' my heart an' my wits, Nick Leary. I saves a woman from a wrack an' brings her into my own house – an' ye names her for a mermaid an' a she-divil! Maybe ye holds wid Dick Lynch 'twas herself kilt the t'ree lads in the cabin – an' her in this house all the time, innocent as a babe."

Leary made the sign of the cross quickly and furtively.

"Nay, skipper; but the divil was in that wrack," he said. "The lads got to fightin' over the gold, skipper, an' Dick Lynch slipped his knife into Pat Brennen. Sure, the divil come ashore from that wrack. Never afore did them two pull their knives on each other; an' now Pat Brennen lays bleedin' his life out. The divil bes got into the lads o' Chance Along, nary a doubt, an' the black luck has come to the harbor."

"The divil an' the black luck bes in their own stinkin' hearts!" exclaimed Nolan, violently.

"Aye, skipper; but they says it bes her ye brought ashore put the curse on to us – an' now they bes comin' this way, skipper, to tell ye to run her out o' yer house."

"What d'ye say?" cried the skipper, springing from his chair. "Run her out, ye say?"

He trembled with fury, burned the air with oaths, and called down all the curses known to tradition upon the heads of the men of Chance Along. He snatched up a stout billet of birch, green and heavy, wrenched open the door, and sprang into the outer gloom.

Nick Leary's story was true. The mutineers had consumed the brandy, come to hot words over the sharing of the gold, dropped their dead and wounded, and commenced to curse, kick and hit at one another with clubs. Then Dick Lynch had put his knife into a young man named Pat Brennen, a nephew of the loyal Bill. Panic had brought the fight to a drunken, slobbering finish.

"There bes four strong lads kilt in one day!" some one had cried. "The black curse bes on us! The divil bes in it!"

Full of liquor, fear and general madness, they had come to the opinion that the strange young female whom the skipper had saved from the foretop and carried to his house was such an imp of darkness as had never before blighted the life and luck of Chance Along. She had bewitched the skipper. Her evil eyes had cast a curse on the wreck and that curse had been the death of their three comrades. She had put a curse on the gold, so that they had all gone mad the moment they felt the touch of it in their hands. The skipper, under her spell, had betrayed them — had given them gold so that they should fight over it and destroy one another. It was all very simple — too simple to require reasoning! In truth, the curse was upon them — the curse of dead men's liquor, dead men's gold — the curse of greed, bloodlust and fear! So they had picked up their dead, their wounded and their loot and continued their journey at top speed, intent on casting out the witch, and bringing the skipper to a knowledge of his desperate state even if the operation should cost him his life. What cared they for his life now that he had lost his luck?

They reached Chance Along, scattered for a few minutes to dispose of the dead and wounded, gathered again and crowded toward the skipper's house. They were quiet now, for the superstitious fear had not entirely driven from their hearts the human fear of the skipper's big hands and terrible eyes. They stumbled and reeled against one another, their heads and feet muddled by brandy and excitement. Some were armed with sticks, a few had drawn their knives, others had forgotten to arm themselves with anything. They trod upon each other's feet in the dark, narrow, uneven ways between the cabins. Bill Brennen joined them in the dark. He carried a broken oar of seasoned ash in his hands. He had sent Nick Leary to warn the skipper of the approach of the mutineers; and his faith in the skipper's prowess was such that he felt but little anxiety. He was sober and he knew that Black Dennis Nolan was sober. He kept to the rear of the mob, just far enough behind it to allow for a full swing of his broken oar, and waited for his master to make the first move against this disorderly demonstration of superstition, bottle-valor and ingratitude. He removed his mittens, stowed them in his belt and spat upon the palms of his hands while he waited. Being sober, he reasoned. Bad luck had struck the harbor this day, beyond a doubt, and brought death and mutiny. But death had not come to the skipper. Not so much as a scratch had come to the skipper. If a witch was in the harbor he trusted to Black Dennis Nolan to deal with her without bringing harm upon himself or his friends. If the devil himself visited Chance Along he would look to the skipper to outwit, outcurse and out-devil him. This is how he felt about the man he had attached himself to. He gripped his broken oar with his moistened palm and fingers and waited hopefully. He had not long to wait.

Suddenly the door of the skipper's house flew open and out of the glow of candle-light leaped a figure that might easily (under the circumstances and condition of the mob) have been the devil himself – himself, the father of all the little devils in hell. The wrathful bellow of him was like the roar of a wounded walrus. He touched ground in the centre of the front rank of the mob, and as his feet touched the ground his billet of green birch cracked down upon a skull. And still he continued to roar; and still the club cracked and cracked; and then Bill Brennen got heartily to work on the rear rank with his broken oar.

The mob of mutineers had arrived intoxicated, and with no very clear idea of what they intended to do to the witch and the skipper. They had intended to make the first move, however; of that they were certain. They had intended to open the door themselves – and now some divil had opened it before they were ready! They were so unsteady on their feet that no man of them stood up for a second blow. A few got to work on their own account; but it was so dark that they did little damage even to their friends. After five or six had fallen the next in order for treatment faced about to retire. In their indignation and bewilderment they discovered that another club was at work in their rear. This unnerved them so that they – the survivors of the demonstration – raised their voices to heaven in expostulation and stampeded. They went over Bill Brennen like a wave over a bar, knocking the breath out of him, and sending the oar flying from his grasp; but the skipper kept right after them, still roaring, still plying the billet of green birch. They scattered, each dashing for his own cabin, bursting open the door, sprawling inside, and shutting the door with his feet.

After the last door had been slammed in his face, the skipper went home. He found Bill Brennen seated by the stove, trying a pipeful of Mother Nolan's tobacco. He had regained his broken oar and held it tenderly across his knees.

"We sure put the witchery into them squid, skipper, sir," he said. "We sure larned 'em the black magic, by Peter!"

T HE SKIPPER kept his two unswerving henchmen to supper and brewed a mighty bowl in their honor. He even condescended to thank Nick for his warning, roundabout and prolonged though it had been, and to throw a word of praise to Bill Brennen. He felt that the unqualified success of his unexpected attack upon the mob had rewon for him much of his mastery of the harbor. The others agreed with him. Bill Brennen, with a mug full of punch in his hand, and his eyes on the broken oar which had stood in a corner, humbly advised him to bestir himself at an early hour in the morning, and put the finishing touches on the lesson. He advised a house-to-house visitation before the heroes had recovered from the brandy and the birch billet – not to mention the oar.

"Bat 'em agin whilst their heads bes still sore," said Bill – which is only another and more original way of saying, "Strike while the iron is hot."

"When ye give 'em all the money, skipper, they sure t'ought ye was bewitched," said Nick Leary. "They t'ought ye was under a spell – an' next they was t'inkin' as how the gold sure had a curse on to it or ye wouldn't give it to 'em."

The skipper nodded. "I was too easy wid 'em!" he said. "Sure, b'ys, I'll be mendin' it."

Bill and Nick departed at last; Cormick ascending the ladder to his bed in the loft; Mother Nolan brewed a dose of herbs of great virtue – she was wise in such things – and still the skipper sat by the stove and smoked his pipe. Never before had his life known another such day as this. Now he could have sworn that a whole month had passed since he had been awakened by news of the wreck under the cliff, and again it seemed as swift and dazzling as the flash of the powder in the pan of his old sealing-gun when the spark flies from the flint. It had certainly been an astonishing day! He had saved a life. He had seen those wonderful, pale lids blink open and the soul sweep back into those wonderful eyes. He had been elbow to elbow with violent death. He had struggled submerged in water tinged with blood. He had

Some Early Visits 81

known exultation, anger and something which a less courageous man would have accepted for defeat. He had suffered a mutiny – and later, in a few violent, reckless minutes of action he had broken it – or cowed it at least. Now he felt himself master of the harbor again, but not the master of his own destiny. He did not sum up his case in these terms; but this is what it came to. Destiny was a conviction with him, and not a word at all – a nameless conviction. He did not consider the future anew; but he felt, without analyzing it, a breathless, new curiosity of what the morrow might hold for him. This sensation was in connection with the girl. Apart from her, his old plans and ambitions stood. He felt no uncertainty and no curiosity concerning the morrow's dealings with the men. He considered it a commonplace subject. He would act upon Bill Brennen's advice and visit the mutineers at an early hour; and as to the wreck? – well, if conditions proved favorable he would break out the cargo and see what could be made of it.

Mother Nolan entered with an empty cup in her hand.

"She took her draught like a babe, an' bes sleepin' agin peaceful as an angel," she whispered. "Mind ye makes no noise, Denny. No more o' yer fightin' an' cursin' this night!"

Black Dennis Nolan put in a night of disturbed dreaming and crawled from his bed before the first streak of dawn. He pulled on his heavy garments and seal-hide "skinnywoppers," built up the fire in the stove, brewed and gulped a mug of tea, and then unbolted the door noiselessly and went out. The dawn was lifting by now, clear, glass-gray and narrow at the rim of the sea to the eastward and southward. The air was still. The lapping of the tide along the icy land-wash and the dull whispering of it among the seaward rocks were the only sounds. The skipper stood motionless beside his own door for a few minutes. Small windows blinked alight here and there; faint, muffled sounds of awakening life came to him from the cabins; pale streamers of smoke arose into the breathless air from the little chimneys.

"Now I'll pay me calls on 'em, like good Father McQueen himself," murmured the skipper.

He moved across the frosty rock to the nearest door. It was opened to him by a wide-eyed woman with a ragged shawl thrown over her head.

"Mornin' to ye, Kate. How bes yer man Tim this mornin'?" inquired the skipper.

He stepped inside without waiting for an answer or an invitation. He found Tim in the bed beside the stove, snoring heavily. He grabbed his shoulder and shook it roughly until the fellow closed his mouth and opened his eyes.

"Tim Leary, ye squid, shut off yer fog-horn an' hark to me!" he exclaimed. "By sun-up ye goes back to the woods and commences cuttin' out poles for Father McQueen's church. Ye'll take yer brother Corny an' Peter Walen along wid ye an' ye'll chop poles all day. Mark that, Tim. I let ye take a fling yesterday, jist to see what kind o' dogs ye be; but if ever I catches ye takin' another widout the word from me I'll be killin' ye!"

The man groaned.

"Holy saints, skipper, ye'd not be sendin' me to choppin' poles wid a head on me like a lobster-pot?" he whispered. "Sure, skipper, me poor head feels that desperate bad, what wid the liquor an' the clout ye give me, I couldn't heave it up from the pillow if Saint Peter himself give the word."

"I bain't troublin' about Saint Peter," returned the skipper. "If ever he wants ye to chop poles he'll see as how ye does it, I bes t'inkin'! It bes me a-tellin' ye now; an' if ye can't carry yer head to the woods wid ye to-day, ye treacherous dog, I'll knock it off for ye to-night so ye'll be able to carry it 'round in yer two hands. Mark that!"

So the skipper paid his round of morning calls. At some cabins he paused only long enough to shout a word through the door, at others he remained for several minutes, re-inspiring treacherous but simple hearts with the fear of Dennis Nolan, master of Chance Along. At one bed he stayed for fifteen minutes, examining and rebandaging the wound given by the knife of Dick Lynch. As for that drunken, sullen, treacherous savage, Dick Lynch himself, he dragged him from his blankets, knocked him about the floor, and then flung him back on to his bed. Then, turning to the dazed man's horrified wife, he said, "See that he don't turn on me agin, Biddy, or by the crowns o' the Holy Saints I'll be the everlastin' death o' him!"

At some of the cabins his orders were for the woods, and at some they were for work on the stranded ship. He did not disturb Bill Brennen or Nick Leary. He knew that they would be around at his house for orders by sun-up. The last cabin he visited was that of Pat Kavanagh. Kavanagh was a man of parts, and had been a close friend of the old skipper. He was a man of the world, having sailed deep-sea voyages in his youth. He was a grand fiddler, a grand singer, and had made more "Come-all-ye's" than you could count on your fingers and toes. He had a wooden leg; and his daughter was the finest girl in Chance Along. His best known Come-all-ye, which is sung to this day from Caplin Arm to Bay Bulls, starts like this:

> Come, all ye hardy fisher-men
>   An' hearken to me lay
> O' how the good brig "Peggy Bell"
>   Went down in Trin'ty Bay.
>
> The skipper he was from St. John's,
>   The mate from Harbor Grace;
> The bosun was a noble lad
>   Wid whiskers 'round his face.

Pat Kavanagh was the author of the ballad that commences this way, and of many more.

He was proud of his daughter and his wooden leg; he was happy with his fiddle and his verses; he did not hold with physical or emotional violence, and asked the world for nothing more than to be left alone beside his stove with a knowledge that there was something in the pot and a few cakes of hard bread in the bin. He could not understand the new skipper, his terrible activity, his hard-fisted ways and his ambitions, and he took no stock in wrecks except as subjects for songs; but he had been delighted with a gift of four fine blankets and two quarts of rum which the skipper had made him recently.

Mary Kavanagh opened the door to the skipper, and let a fine light slip into her blue eyes at the sight of him. Her cheeks, which had been unusually pale when she opened the door, flushed bright and deep. The young man greeted her pleasantly and easily, and stepped across the threshold. Pat was already out of bed and seated in his chair close to the stove. He was long and thin, with a straggling beard and moustaches, a long face, a long nose, and kindly, twinkling eyes. Though he looked happy enough he also looked like a widower – why, I can't say. It may have been owing to his general unstowed, unfurled, un-swabbed appearance. He had not yet fastened on his wooden leg. He never did, nowadays, until he had eaten his breakfast and played a tune or two on his fiddle. His eyes were paler than his daughter's, and not nearly so bright, and he had a way

of staring at a thing for minutes at a time as if he did not see it
– and usually he didn't. Altogether, he was a very impractical
person. He must have made a feeble sailor – a regular fool as a
look-out – and the wonder is that he lost only one leg during his
deep-sea career. He looked at the skipper with that calm, far-
away shimmer in his eyes, combing his thin whiskers with his
fingers. He did not speak. His wooden leg was leaning up against
his chair.

"Good morning to ye, Pat Kavanagh," said the skipper.

The poet blinked his eyes, thereby altering their expression
from a shimmer to a gray, wise gleam.

"So it bes yerself, Skipper Denny," he said. "Set down. Set
down. Sure, b'y, I didn't expect to see ye so spry to-day, an' was
just studyin' out a few verses concernin' death an' pride an'
ructions that would keep yer memory green."

"Whist, father!" exclaimed the girl.

"I bain't dead, Pat, so ye kin set to on some new varses," said
the skipper. "If ye t'ought them poor fools ye heard yowlin'
last night was to be the death o' me, then ye was on the wrong
tack. But I bes here now to ax yer opinion concernin' them
same fools, Pat. Yesterday they raised a mutiny agin me, all
along o' a poor girl as I saved from the wrack, an' last night an'
this mornin' I larned 'em the error o' their ways. Now ye was
once a deep-sea sailorman, Pat, a-sailin' foreign v'yages, an' so I
wants ye to tell me what I'd better be doin' wid some o' them
squid? There was Foxey Jack Quinn; but he run away an' done
for himself in the flurry. Here bes Dick Lynch, nigh as treacherous an' full o' divilment as ever Jack was, growlin' an' snarlin'
at me heels like a starvin' husky an' showin' his teeth every now
an' agin. So I wants to know, Pat, will I kill him dead or run him
out o' the harbor? I bes skipper here – aye, an' more nor skipper – an' all a man has to do to live safe an' happy an' rich in
this harbor bes to do what I tells him to do – but this here Dick
Lynch bain't knowledgeable enough to see it. I's had to bat him
twice. Next time I bats him maybe I'd best finish the job? I puts
it to ye, Pat Kavanagh, because ye knows the world an' how
sich things bes done aboard foreign-going ships."

"This harbor bain't no foreign-going ship, Denny," replied the
poet.

"True, Pat; but if I calls it a ship it bes the same as one!"
retorted the skipper.

"If ye takes it that way, Denny, then ye'd best be handin' the lad over to the jedges to be tried for mutiny," suggested the other, quietly. "But if ye wants my opinion, ye'll leave him be."

"Leave him be?"

"Aye. He bain't worth troublin' about. Bat him now an' agin, if he tries to knife ye, an' maybe he'll follow Jack Quinn. But this harbor bain't a ship, lad. The skipper o' a ship has the law to his back in cases o' mutiny an' the like — but the law bain't behind ye, Dennis Nolan!"

"The divil fly away wid the law!" cried the skipper. "I bes skipper here! I makes the law for this harbor — an' them as don't like the laws I makes kin go somewheres else."

"Leave him be, skipper. That bes what I tells ye, for yer own good. Don't kill him. Ye kin break up desarted wracks; ye kin fill yer pockets wid gold; ye kin bat yer mates over the nob if ye wants to; but once ye gets to killin' men, Denny Nolan, then ye'll find the law to yer back sure enough, a-fixin' a noose around yer neck! Aye, lad, that bes the truth! I warns ye because I likes ye — an' I bes glad to see ye so prosperous."

x   Mary Kavanagh

A NUMBER OF men with sore heads and dry mouths made their way to the top of the cliff, across the barrens and into a thin belt of spruces. There they worked as well as they could at cutting timber for Father McQueen's church. They were a dolorous company. The daring spirit of mutiny had passed away, leaving behind it the fear of the skipper. The courage, uplift and inspiring glow of the brandy had ebbed and evaporated, leaving the quaking stomach, the swimming brain, the misty eye. They groaned as they hacked at the trees, for the desire to lie down on the cold snow was heavy upon them; but still they hacked away, for the fear of Black Dennis Nolan, the unconquerable, was like a hot breath upon their necks. They said some bitter things about Dick Lynch.

The skipper visited the wreck, accompanied by Bill Brennen and a few of the men and boys who had not taken part in yesterday's mutiny. The sea was almost flat and there was no wind. The hatches were broken open; and what they could see of the *Royal William*'s cargo looked entirely satisfactory to them – sail-cloth, blankets, all manner of woollen and cotton goods, boots and shoes, hams, cheeses and tinned meats. Though some of these things were damaged by the salt water, few of them were ruined by it. They worked all day at winching out the cargo. Next day, the men who had cooled their sore heads in the woods were also put to work on the stranded ship. With timbers and tarpaulins from the ship they built a store-house on the barren, in the midst of a thicket of spruces. In the two days they managed to save about a quarter of the cargo. The skipper drove them hard, an iron belaying pin in his hand and slashing words always on his lips. But even the dullest of them saw that he neither drove, cursed nor threatened Bill Brennen, Nick Leary or any of the men who had kept out of the mutiny. Most of the stuff that was salvaged was put in the new store, but a few hundreds of pounds of it were carried to the harbor.

During these two days the skipper did not once set eyes on the girl he had saved from the fore-top. Mother Nolan would not let him approach within two yards of the door of the room in which she lay. It seemed, from Mother Nolan's talk, that the beautiful stranger was always sleeping. But, through the old woman, he learned her name. It was Flora Lockhart.

When the skipper and Cormick reached home after the second day's work on the cargo, Mother Nolan told them that Flora was in the grip of a desperate fever, upon which none of her brews of roots and herbs seemed to have any effect. She was hot as fire and babbled continually of things strange and mad to the ears of the old woman. The skipper was dismayed at the news; but his vigorous mind immediately began to search for a means of dealing with the fever. He knew nothing of any remedies save the local ones, in the manufacture and administering of which his grandmother was a mistress. But here was the *Royal William*'s medicine-chest, and here was Pat Kavanagh who had sailed foreign voyages in vessels carrying similar chests. He rushed from the house straight to the poet-fiddler's cabin. He pushed open the door and entered without knocking, as the custom is in Chance Along. Mary was attending to a stew-pan on the stove, and Pat was seated in his chair with his wooden leg strapped in place. The skipper told of the stranger's fever.

"An' ye has the ship's medicine-chest?' queried Pat. "Then we'll give her the bitter white powder – quinine – aye, quinine. Every ship carries it, lad. When I was took wid the fever in Port-o'-Spain didn't the mate shake it on to me tongue till me ears crackled like hail on the roof, an' when I got past stickin' out me tongue didn't he mix it wid whiskey an' pour it into me? Sure, Denny! An' it knocked the fever galley west in t'ree days an' left me limp as cook's dish-clout hangin' to dry under the starboard life-boat. But it bes better nor dyin' entirely wid the fever. I'll step round wid ye, skipper, and p'int out this here quinine to ye."

And he did. He found a large bottle of quinine in the box, in powder form. He measured out a quantity of it in doses of from three to five grains, for his memory of the sizes of the doses administered to him by the mate was somewhat dim, and advised Mother Nolan not to give the powders too often nor yet not often enough. Mother Nolan asked for more exact directions. She felt that she had a right to them. Pat Kavanagh combed his long whiskers reflectively with his long fingers, gazing at the medicine-chest with a far-away look in his pale eyes.

"I don't rightly recollect the ins an' outs o' me own case," he said, at last, "but I has a dim picter in me mind o' how Mister Swim, the mate, shook the powder on to me tongue every blessed time I opened me mouth to holler. An' the b'ys let me drink all the cold water I could hold – aye, an' never once did they wake me up when I was sleepin' quiet, not even to give the quinine to me. An' they stowed me in blankets an' made me sweat, though the fo'castle was hotter nor the hatches o' hell. An' when I wouldn't stick out me tongue for the powder then they'd melt it in whiskey an' pour it down me neck."

With this Mother Nolan had to be content. She retired to her own room, mixed a powder in a cup of root-tea and gave it to the girl, who was quiet now, though wide-awake and bright-eyed. Kavanagh went home, invented a ballad about his fever in Port-o'-Spain, and wrote it upon his memory, verse by verse – for he did not possess the art of writing upon paper. After supper Cormick retired to the loft and his bed; but the skipper did not touch a blanket that night. He spent most of the time in his chair by the stove; but once in every hour he tiptoed into his grandmother's room and listened. If he heard any sound from the inner room when the old woman happened to be asleep he awakened her and sent her in to Flora Lockhart. At dawn he fell asleep in his chair and dreamed that he was the mate of a foreign-going ship, and that all he had to do was to shake white powders on to the tongue of the girl he had saved from the fore-top of the *Royal William*. Cormick shook him awake when breakfast was ready. After hearing from Mother Nolan that the girl seemed much cooler and better than she had since the early afternoon of the previous day, he ate his breakfast and went out and sent all the able-bodied men to get timber for Father McQueen's church, some from the woods and others from the wreck. They would haul the timber after the next fall of snow. But he did not go abroad himself. He hung about the harbor all day, sometimes in his own kitchen, sometimes down on the land-wash, and sometimes in other men's cabins. He put a new dressing on the wound of the lad who had received the knife and paid another visit to Dick Lynch. Lynch was still in bed; but this time he did not drag him out on the floor.

Mother Nolan was full of common sense and wise instincts, in spite of the fact that she believed in fairies, mermaids and the personal attentions of the devil. She was doctor and nurse by nature as well as by practice – by everything, in short, but education. So it happened that she did not follow Pat Kavanagh's instructions to the letter. She argued to herself that Pat's fever had been a hot-climate one, while Flora Lockhart's was undoubtedly a cold-climate one. She saw that the girl's trouble was a sickness, accompanied by high fever, brought on by cold and exposure. So she did not give the quinine quite as generously as the fiddler had recommended, and kept right on with her hot brews of herbs and roots in addition. Instinct told her that if she could drive out the cold the fever would follow it out of its own accord.

In the afternoon the girl became restless and highly feverish again, and by sunset she was slightly delirious. She talked constantly in her wonderful voice of fame, of great cities and of many more things which sounded meaningless and alarming to Mother Nolan. For a little while she thought she was on the *Royal William*, talking to the captain about the great reception that awaited her in New York, her own city, which she had left four years ago, humble and unknown, and was now returning to, garlanded with European recognition. It was all double-Dutch to Mother Nolan. She put an end to it with her potent dose of quinine and whiskey. She spent this night in her patient's room, keeping the fire roaring and catching cat-naps in a chair by the hearth; and the skipper haunted the other side of the door. Toward morning the girl asked for a drink, as sanely as anybody could, took it eagerly, and then sank into a quiet sleep. The old woman nodded in her chair. The skipper tiptoed back to the kitchen and flung himself across his bed.

After the fourth day of the fight against the fever Mother Nolan saw that the struggle was likely to prove too much for her, if prolonged at the present pitch, whatever it might prove for Flora Lockhart; so she sent the skipper over to bring Mary Kavanagh to her. Now Mary was as kind-hearted and honest as she was big and beautiful. Her mind was strong and sane, and spiced with a quick wit. Her kindness and honesty were spiced with a warm temper. She was human all through. As she could flame to love so could she flame to anger. As she could melt to pity so could she chill to pride. In short, though she was a fine and good young woman, she wasn't an angel. Angels have their place in heaven; and the place and duty of Mary Kavanagh was on this poor earth, where men's souls are still held in shells of clay and wrenched this way and that way by the sorrows and joys of their red hearts. Like most good human women, Mary had all the makings of a saint in her; but heaven itself could never make a sexless, infallible angel of her.

Mary told her father not to forget to keep the fire burning, threw a blue cloak over her head and shoulders, and accompanied the skipper back to Mother Nolan. Short as the distance was between the two dwellings she glanced twice at her companion, with kindliness, inquiry and something of anxiety in her dark gray eyes. But he stared ahead of him so intently, with eyes somewhat haggard from lack of sleep, that he did not notice the glances. Mother Nolan welcomed her joyfully.

"Help me tend on this poor lamb from the wrack," said the old woman, "an' ye'll be the savin' of me life. Me poor old eyes feels heavy as stove-lids, Mary dear."

"Sure, I'll help ye, Mother Nolan, an' why not?" returned Mary, throwing aside her cloak from her smooth brown head and strong, shapely shoulders. "Father kin mind himself, if he bes put to it, for a little while. Now tell me what ye does for the lady, Mother Nolan, dear, an' give me a look at her, an' then pop into bed wid ye, an' I'll lay a bottle o' hot water to yer feet."

"Saints bless ye, me dear. May every hair o' yer darlint head turn into a wax candle to light ye to glory amongst the holy saints," returned the old woman.

So it came about that Mary Kavanagh joined in the fight for the life of the girl from the wreck. She stood her trick at Flora's bedside turn and turn about with the old woman, quiet as a fairy on her feet, though she was surely as big as a dozen fairies, quiet as a whisper with her voice, her hands as gentle as snow that falls in windless weather. She did not worry about her father. There was bread in the bin and fish in the shed for him, and he had his fiddle and his ballads. Every evening, sometimes before and sometimes after supper, he came over and sat with the skipper, combing his long beard with his restless fingers, and telling improbable tales of his deep-sea voyages.

The skipper's faith in his grandmother and Mary was great. He soon schooled himself to stay away from the house for hours at a time, and give at least half his attention to the work of impressing the men with his mastery, and getting out lumber for the little church which Father McQueen was to build in June, on the barrens behind and above Chance Along. The men felt and knew his touch of mastery. They felt that this work at church-building was sure to lift any curse and devilment from the harbor, if such things had really been, and establish the skipper's good luck for all time. Dick Lynch, who still walked feebly, with a bandage about his head, was in bad repute with all of them, and more especially with the blood-kin of the young man whom he had knifed in the drunken fight over the gold. But the youth who had been knifed, Pat Brennen by name, was in a fair way to recover from the wound, thanks to the skipper's care and the surgical dressings from the *Royal William's* medicine-chest. So they worked well, ate well, clothed themselves in warm garments made by their womenfolk from the goods saved from the last wreck, and said with their undependable tongues, from the shallows of their undependable hearts, that Black Dennis Nolan was a great man and a terrible. The spirit of distrust and revolt was dead – or sound asleep, at least.

The hot poison of the fever in Flora Lockhart's blood was drawn after days of ceaseless care and innumerable doses of quinine and brews of herbs and roots; but it left behind it a weakness of spirit and body, and a dangerous condition of chest and throat. Mother Nolan and Mary Kavanagh saw that the fight was only half won, and neither of them laid aside their arms for a moment, though they changed their tactics. Now the fire in the chimney was kept roaring more fiercely than ever, bottles of hot water were kept always in the bed, the blankets were heated freely, and hot broth and steaming spirits were given in place of the brews of roots and leaves. The skipper and Cormick went far afield and succeeded in shooting several willow-grouse, and these Mother Nolan made into broth for Flora. The best of everything that could be procured was hers. She began to recover strength at last, and then each day brought improvement. By this time she and Mary Kavanagh had warmed toward each other until a friendship was established. Flora had thanked Mary beautifully, many times over, for her care, and had talked a great deal of herself and her ambitions. She had told Mary and Mother Nolan the hardships and glories of her past and her great dreams for the future. On the day that Mary was to go back to her father, Flora drew her down and kissed her fondly.

"You and Mother Nolan have saved my life," she said, "and I am your friend – yours especially, Mary – forever and ever. I shall prove my love and gratitude, you may be sure. Out in the big world, Mary, I am *somebody* – I have the power to do kindnesses and repay debts. New York is full of fame and money, and a great deal of it is waiting for me."

Mary thanked her, kissed her in return, and said gently that she did not want to be rewarded for her nursing, except by love. She added that it was Black Dennis Nolan, the skipper, who had saved Flora's life.

"I remember him vaguely," said the other. "He took me away from that terrible place where I was swaying and tossing between the waves and the sky. The queer things I saw in my fever dreams have dimmed the memory of the wreck, thank God – and now they themselves are growing dim. He is a big man, is he not, and young and very strong? And his eyes are almost black, I think. I will pay him for what he has done, you may be sure, Mary. I suppose he is a fisherman, or something of that kind?"

"He bain't the kind to want money for what he has done," said Mary, slowly. "He be skipper o' Chance Along, like his father was afore him – but there never was another skipper like him, for all that. He saved ye from the wrack, an' now ye lay in his house – but I warns ye not to offer money to him for the sarvice he has done ye. Sure, he wouldn't be needin' the money, an' wouldn't take it if he was. He lives by the sea – aye, in his own way! – an' when the sea feeds full at all she fills her men with the divil's own pride."

Flora was puzzled and slightly amused. She patted the other's hand and smiled up at her.

"Is he so rich then?" she asked. "And what is a skipper? – if he is not the captain of a ship? How can a man be the skipper of a village like this?"

"His father was skipper," replied Mary. "The fore-an'-aft schooner bes his, an' the store wid flour an' tea in it for who-ever needs them. It bes the way o' the coast – more or less."

"Have any letters come for me? Have people from New York arranged yet to take me away?" asked Flora, suddenly forgetting about the skipper and remembering her own career so terribly interrupted and so strangely retarded. "I shall be able to travel in a few days, I think. What have the newspapers said about my misfortunes?"

The pink faded a little from Mary's cheeks and her gray eyes seemed to dim.

"Saints love ye!" she said. "There bes no letters for ye, my dear – an' how would there be? Up-along they'll be still waitin' for the ship – or maybe they have give up waitin' by this time. How would they know she was wracked on this coast?"

The beautiful singer gazed at her in consternation and amazement. Her wonderful sea-eyes flashed to their clear sea-depths where the crosslights lay.

"But – but has no word been sent to New York? – to any-where?" she cried. "Surely you cannot mean that people do not know of the wreck, and that I am here? What of the owners of the ship? Oh, God, what a place!"

Mary was startled for a moment, then thoughtful. She had never before wondered what the great world of "Up-along" – which is everywhere south and east and west of Newfoundland, London, New York, Pernambuco, Halifax, Montreal, Africa, China and the lands and seas around and between – must think of the ships that sail away and never return. Wrecks had always seemed to her as natural as tides and storms. When the tide comes in who thinks of reporting it to the great world? Spars and shattered timbers come in on the tides; and sometimes hulls more or less unbroken; and sometimes living humans. Mary had seen something of these things herself and had heard much. She had never known of the spars or hulls being claimed by any person but the folk who found them and fought with the sea for them. She had seen shipwrecked sailors tarry awhile, take their food thankfully, and presently set out for St. John's and the world beyond, by way of Witless Bay. None of them had ever come back to Chance Along.

"I bes sorry for ye wid my whole heart," she said. "Yer folks will be mournin' for ye, I fear – for how would they know ye was safe in Chance Along? But the saints have presarved your life, dear, an' when spring-time comes then ye can sail 'round to St. John's an' away to New York. But sure, we might have writ a letter about ye an' carried it out to Witless Bay. The skipper can write."

"I have been buried alive!" cried Flora, covering her face with her hands and weeping unrestrainedly.

Mary tried to comfort her, then left the room to find Mother Nolan. The old woman was in the kitchen, and Dennis was with her.

"She bes desperate wrought-up because – because her folks up-along will think she bes dead," explained Mary. "She says she bes buried alive in Chance Along. Skipper, ye had best write a letter about herself an' the wrack, an' send it out. She bes a great person up-along."

The skipper sprang to his feet, staring at her with a blank face and with defiance in his eyes.

"A letter!" he exclaimed, huskily. "No, by hell! Let 'em t'ink what they wants to! Bain't Chance Along good enough for her?"

MARY KAVANAGH paled, flushed again, and lowered her eyes. Old Mother Nolan turned a searching glance upon her grandson – a glance with derision and something of pity in it.

"An' how would Chance Along be good enough for the likes o' her?" said she. "Denny Nolan, bes ye a fool entirely? Good enough for her, says ye – an' her singin' like a lark afore the young Queen herself, saints presarve her, wid the Prince an' the dukes a-settin' round in their grand gold crowns, a-trowin' roses an' jewels at her little feet! What bes Chance Along to her – aye, an' any poor soul in it? We've give her life back to her, Denny, me lad, an' now we'll give herself back to the grand world o' up-along, where great singers bes nigh the same as great ladies, as I have heard me own grandfather tell, who was once in Dublin a-holdin' the gentry's horses at the play-house door."

The skipper glared straight before him, then sank into his chair.

"I'll pen no letter," he said, "I swears it by the knuckle-bones o' the holy saints!"

Mother Nolan turned to Mary, wagging her head.

"There bes ink an' a pen on the shelf there, an' a scrap o' clean paper in Denny's great book yonder," she said. "Take 'em to her an' let her pen the word wid her own hand." She turned to Denny. "And ye, Denny Nolan, will send it out to Witless Bay, an' from Witless Bay to St. John's, an' so to New York."

"I hears ye," returned the skipper.

"Aye, that ye do," said the spirited old woman, "an' a good t'ing for ye I bes here to tell ye! Why for wouldn't ye be sendin' out the letter? What for d'ye be wantin' Miss Flora Lockhart to stop here in Chance Along? – and her who never put a hand to a stroke o' honest work since her mother bore her! – her who sang to the Queen o' England! Ye'd be better, Denny, wid a real true mermaid, tail an' all, in Chance Along. Wrack ye kin break abroad; cargoes ye kin lift an' devour; gold an' jewels ye kin hide away; but when live women be t'rowed up to ye by the sea ye kin do naught but let 'em go. The divil bes in the women, lad – the women from up-along. An' the law would be on yer heels – aye, an' on to yer neck – afore ye knowed how the wind was blowin'! An' what would his riverence be sayin' to ye?"

Mary Kavanagh had left the kitchen by this time, carrying pen, ink and paper to the girl in Father McQueen's room. Denny raised his head, and met the regard of his grandmother's bright old eyes proudly.

"I wants to marry her," he said. "An' why not? Bain't I skipper here – aye, skipper o' every man an' boat in the harbor? She'd have no call to touch her hand to honest work if she was my wife. Bain't I rich? – and like to be richer? I'll build her a grand house. She'll have wine every day, an' jewels on her fingers, an' naught to do all day, by Saint Peter, but put the gowns o' silk on to her back. Bain't that better nor singin' an' cavortin' afore the Queen?"

"Denny, ye bes a fool, sure, for all yer great oaths an' masterful ways wid the men," said Mother Nolan. "Ye bes a fool over a woman – an' that be the weakest kind o' fool! What would a lady like her be wantin' wid ye for a husband? – wid a ignorant great fisherman the like o' ye, skipper o' no skipper? What bes a skipper to the like o' her? No more nor a dog, Denny Nolan! She'd break yer heart an' send yer soul to damnation!"

The skipper left his chair without a word, and strode from the kitchen to Mother Nolan's own room, stooping as he passed through the low doorway. He advanced until he reached Flora's room. It was shut. He halted for a moment, breathing quickly, then rapped with his knuckles, and opened the door. Flora was sitting upright in the bed, backed by pillows and with a shawl over her shoulders. She had been writing; and Mary stood beside the bed and held the bottle of time-faded ink for her. Both girls looked up with startled faces at the skipper's entrance. The young man halted in the middle of the room, and stared at the singer. It was the first time he had seen her since the day he had saved her from the *Royal William*'s fore-top and brought her to this house. He saw that her face was thinner now than on that day, but no paler. The wonderful eyes were as clear, as bright as crystal, and yet as limpid, as when they had first opened to him, there on the swaying cross-trees, and worked their spell on him. But the lips were red now – as red and bewitching as a mermaid's lips are supposed to be. She was the first to speak.

"What is it? What do you want?" she asked somewhat fretfully, in that silver voice that had delighted the ears of the young Queen on the other side of the ocean. The question, or perhaps the way it was asked, sent a chill through Black Dennis Nolan. His glance wavered and he crumpled his fur cap in his hands. His sudden confusion showed in his dark face.

"It bes the skipper," said Mary Kavanagh, "him that fetched ye from the wrack."

"Oh, I beg your pardon," said Flora. "Of course I should have remembered your face, and now I do. I am very, very grateful to you for saving my life, and I shall never forget it. I shall do everything in my power to repay you for your courage and kindness, you may be sure; but why did you not send out word that I was here? You knew that I could not do it myself, lying here ill with fever. Perhaps they have grown tired of waiting for me by now, in New York. Perhaps they think I am dead. Perhaps they have forgotten me – and that would be worse than death!"

The skipper felt like a fool, then like a whipped dog. It was this last sensation that sent a wave of choking anger through him. He was not accustomed to it. Had any other woman taken him to task so he would have laughed and forgotten the incident in a minute. Had any man shown such ingratitude he would have smashed his head; but now his dark face flushed and he muttered a few words thickly which passed unheard and unheeded even by himself.

"I am writing now," continued Flora, "and must ask you to send it out to some place from which it can reach civilization, and be mailed to New York. It is very important – almost a matter of life and death to me – for it may yet be in time to save my career, even my engagement in New York."

The skipper maintained his silence, crushing his cap in his big hands and glowering at the rag-mat under his feet. Two kinds of love, several kinds of devils, pride, anger and despair were battling in his heart.

"Ye'll take out the letter, skipper, sure ye will," said Mary, smiling at him across the bed. Her fair face was pink and her eyes perturbed. The man did not notice the pink of her cheeks or the anxiety in her eyes.

"Why, of course you will take it – or send it," said Miss Lockhart. "It is a very small thing to do for a person for whom you have already done so much. You are the kindest people in the world – you three. You have saved my life twice, among you. I shall never, never forget your kindness, and as soon as I reach New York I shall repay you all. I shall soon be rich."

Black Dennis Nolan looked at her, straight into her sea-eyes, and felt the bitter-sweet spell of them again to the very depths of his being. Her glance was the first to waver. A veil of color slipped up softly across her pale cheeks. Young as she was, she had seen other men gaze at her with that same light in their eyes. They had all been young men, she reflected. Others, in Paris and London, had looked with less of pure bewitchment and more of desire in their eyes. She was not ignorant of her charms, her power, her equipment to pluck the pearl from the oyster of the world. She could marry wealth; she could win wealth and more fame with her voice and beauty on the concert-stage; she could do both. But in spite of her knowledge of the great world, her heart was neither blinded to the true things of worth nor entirely hardened. If she ever married, it would be for wealth and position, as the world counted such things, but never a man – lord or commoner – who did not come to her with the light of pure witchery in his eyes. She remembered, smiling down at the half-written letter to her New York agent, how that light had shone in the honest eyes of a young officer of the ship in which she had sailed from America to Europe. Her reflections, which had passed through her brain with a swiftness beyond that of any spoken or written words, were interrupted by the skipper.

"I bes rich now," he said thickly.

Mary Kavanagh lost color at that and turned her face away from them both, toward the fire in the wide chimney. Flora Lockhart looked up at the speaker, puzzled, but still smiling faintly. Her face was very beautiful and kind – but with an elfin kindness that seemed not all womanly, scarcely all human. Her beauty was almost too delicate, striking and unusual to bear the impress of a common-day kindness. She laughed gently but clearly.

"I am glad you are rich," she said. "You are rich in virtues, I know – all three of you."

"I bes rich in gold an' gear," said the skipper. "Rich as any marchant."

"I am glad," returned the girl. "It will be pleasant for me, in the future, to always picture my preservers in comfort. I hope you may continue to prosper, skipper – you and all your people. But here is the letter. How will you get it to New York, do you think?"

The skipper advanced to the bed, and took the letter. His fingers touched hers.

"I'll be takin' it to Witless Bay meself," he stammered. "Sure, that would be safest. It bes a longish trip; but I'll do it." He paused and stared down at the letter in his hand. "But 'twould take me t'ree days an' more, there an' back – an' what would the men be doing wid me away? The divil himself only knows! Maybe they'd get to t'inkin' agin as ye bes a witch. I'll be sendin' Bill Brennen wid it, afore sun-up to-morrow."

"And who will take it from Witless Bay to St. John's?" asked Flora.

"Foxey Garge Hudson, the Queen's own mail-carrier. There bes a post-office in Witless Bay," returned the skipper. "He makes the trip to St. John's once every week in winter-time, bar flurries an' fog, an' maybe twice every week in the summer-time. If it be'd summer-time now I'd sail the letter right round to St. John's in me fore-an'-aft schooner."

"What a terrible place! It seems to be thousands of miles out of the world," murmured the singer. "Don't any ships ever come to this harbor – except wrecks?"

The skipper shook his head. "Me own fore-an'-aft, the *Polly*, bes the only vessel trades wid this harbor," he said. He stowed the letter away in his pocket, turned and strode from the room and out of the house. He looked calm enough now, but the battle was still raging within him.

The skipper was out of bed next morning at the first peep of dawn. He dressed for a long journey, stuffed his pockets with food, and then wakened his grandmother.

"I bes goin' meself wid this letter," he said. "The men won't be tryin' any o' their tricks, I bes t'inkin'. Dick Lynch bain't fit for any divilment yet awhile an' 'tothers be busy gettin' timber for the church. Send Cormy to tell Bill Brennen an' Nick Leary to keep 'em to it."

"Why bes ye goin' yerself, Denny?" inquired the old woman.

"Sure, it bes safest for me to carry the letter, Granny," returned the skipper.

He ate his breakfast, drank three mugs of strong tea, and set out. A little dry snow had fallen during the night. The air was bitterly cold and motionless, and the only sound was the sharp crackling of the tide fingering the ice along the frozen landwash. The sky was clear. With the rising of the sun above the rim of the sea a faint breath of icy wind came out of the west. By this time the skipper was up on the edge of the barrens, a mile and more away from the little harbor. He was walking at a good pace, smoking his pipe and thinking hard. A thing was in his mind that he could not bring himself to face fairly, as yet. It had been with him several hours of yesterday, and all night, and had caused him to change his plan of sending Bill Brennen with the letter – and still it lurked like a shadow in the back of his mind, unilluminated and unproven. But he knew, deep in his heart, that he would presently consider and act upon this lurking, sinister half-thought. Otherwise, he was a fool to be heading for Witless Bay. Bill Brennen, or any other man in the harbor, could have carried the letter as well – except for the idea that had been blindly at work all night in the back of his brain.

He had made four miles of his journey when he halted, turned and looked back along the desolate barrens and the irregular edge of the cliffs. Misgivings assailed him. Was Flora safe? What if something should happen – had already happened, perhaps – to stir his treacherous fellows to mutiny again? Any little accident might do it if they knew that he was on his way to Witless Bay. If one of them should cut his foot with an axe, or drop a tree on one of his comrades, it would be enough (with the skipper out of the way) to raise the suspicion of witchcraft and curses in their silly, mad souls again. And then what would happen? What would happen to Flora, the helpless, wonderful, most beautiful creature in the world. He stared back along his path, but the many curves and breaks in the cliff hid from him every sign of Chance Along. Not a roof, chimney, or streamer of smoke broke the desolation. In all the frozen scene he could find no mark of man or man's handiwork. South and north, east and west, lay the frosted barrens, the gray sea, the edge of the cliff twisting away to nothingness around innumerable lifeless bays and coves, and the far horizons fencing all in a desolate circle. But what mattered to the skipper, what weighed on his heart like despair was the fact that he was out of sight of Chance Along – of the roof that sheltered the girl he had saved from the wreck. He felt the loneliness of that dreary season and coast – for the first time in his life, I think. Anxiety was his teacher.

And now he knew that he must go on to Witless Bay, and so prove himself a fool for not having sent one of the men, or else face and act upon the thought lurking in the back of his mind. He drew the letter from his pocket and looked at it for a long time, turning it over and over between his fur-clad hands.

"She'll soon be forgettin'," he said. "Come summer-time, she'll be forgettin'. I bes rich – an' when she sees the grand house I kin build for her she'll marry me, sure, an' be happy as a queen. An' why not? Bain't I rich as any marchant? She'll be wearin' gold an' silk every day, an' eatin' like any queen – an' bain't that better for a grand lady nor singin' songs for a livin'? – nor singin' songs for her bread an' baccy like old Pat Kavanagh wid the wooden leg?"

He tore the letter to fragments and scattered it upon the snow. He had faced the lurking thought at last and acted upon it.

"Praise be to the saints!" exclaimed the skipper with intense relief. "That bes done – an' a good job, too. That letter'll never be gettin' to up-along, anyhow, an' when she larns how rich I be, an' begins to love me, she'll be praisin' the saints the same as me. Why for would she want to be goin' up-along to New York, anyhow? Now I'll jist shape me course 'round beyant the harbor an' see if they squid be up to any divilment or no."

He made his way inland for about half a mile and then headed southward. As he drew near the line of Chance Along he edged farther away from the coast, deeper into the wilderness of hummocks, frozen bogs and narrow belts of spruce and fir. When at last he heard the axes thumping between himself and the harbor he sat down in a sheltered place and filled and lit his pipe. The men were at work. The letter that would have torn Flora Lockhart from him was not on its way to New York. All was well with the skipper and the world! He remained there for an hour, smoking, listening, congratulating himself. By the thumping of the axes and the slow crashings of falling trees he knew that Bill Brennen had put a big crew at the chopping. This knowledge stilled his anxiety for the girl's safety. He knocked out his pipe and stowed it away and moved farther westward until he found a suitable camping-place behind a wooded hill. Here he made a fire, built a little shelter of poles and spruce branches, and rested at his ease. He thought of Flora Lockhart. Her sea-eyes and red lips were as clear and bright as a picture in his brain. Her wonderful, bell-like voice rang in his ears like fairy music. The spell of her was like a ravishing fire in his heart.

Suddenly the skipper sprang to his feet and slapped a hand on his thigh. He had remembered the necklace for the first time for many days, and with the memory had flashed the thought that with it to offer he would have no difficulty in proving his wealth to the lady and winning her heart. Those white diamonds and red rubies were surely just the things a great lady from up-along would appreciate. Could a king on his throne make her a finer gift? He doubted it. The sight of that necklace would open her eyes and melt her heart to the real worth and greatness of the skipper of Chance Along. Poor Skipper Nolan! But after all, he was little more than a savage. Of the hearts of women – even of the women of Chance Along – he was as ignorant as a spotted harbor-seal. He knew no more of Mary Kavanagh's heart than of Flora Lockhart's, but even a savage may win a heart in ignorance, and even a savage may learn!

With a great oath the skipper vowed that he would find that necklace; but not to sell for gold, as his old intention had been, but to sell for the possession of the girl from up-along. It seemed an easy thing to do. Foxey Jack Quinn could not have gone very far away from the harbor in that "flurry." Perhaps he had turned back and inland, searching blindly for shelter, and lay even now somewhere near this fire? It struck the skipper as a great idea. He would have three clear days to give to the quest of the body of Jack Quinn without arousing the curiosity of the harbor. Three days, as nearly as he could reckon, was the shortest time in which a man could make the journey to Witless Bay and back. As he could not show himself in Chance Along within that time without raising doubts as to the safe delivery of the letter, he was free to devote the time to the recovery of the necklace. It was a grand arrangement altogether. Of course he would keep covertly in touch with the harbor, in case of another panic of superstition; and of course he would find the corpse of Jack Quinn with the precious necklace in its pocket.

B LACK DENNIS NOLAN'S explorations in the wilderness in search of the corpse of Foxey Jack Quinn served no purpose save that of occupying his three days of exile from Chance Along. Of course he acquired a deal of exact information of the country lying beyond the little harbor and north and south of it for several miles; but this knowledge of the minute details of the landscape did not seem of much value to him, at the time. He searched high and low, far and wide, returning at intervals of from three to five hours to within sound of the axes of his men. He dug the dry snow from clefts between granite boulders and ransacked the tangled hearts of thickets of spruce-tuck and alder. He investigated frozen swamps, wooded slopes, rocky knolls and hummocks, and gazed down through black ice at the brown waters of frozen ponds. He carried on his search scientifically, taking his camp as a point of departure and moving away from it in ever widening and lengthening curves. He found the shed antlers of a stag, the barrel of an old, long-lost sealing gun, the skeleton of a caribou, and the bones of a fox with one shank still gripped in the jaws of a rusty trap. He found a large dry cave in the side of a knoll. He found the charred butts of an old camp-fire and near it that which had once been a plug of tobacco – a brown, rotten mass, smelling of dead leaves and wet rags. He found a rusted fish-hook, so thorough was his search – aye, and a horn button. In such signs he read the fleeting history of the passing of generations of men that way – of men from Chance Along who had sought in this wilderness for flesh for their pots and timber for their huts, boats and stages. He found everything but what he was looking for – the frozen body of Foxey Jack Quinn with the necklace of diamonds and rubies in its pocket. Then a haunting fear came to him that the thief had escaped – had won out to the big world in spite of the storm and by some other course than Witless Bay.

With this fear in him, he carried on terribly for a few minutes, raging around his fire, cursing the name and the soul of Foxey Jack Quinn, calling upon the saints for justice, confounding his luck and his enemies. He stopped it suddenly, for he had a way of regaining command of his threshing passions all at once. He did not have to let them thresh themselves out, as is the case with weaker men; but he gripped them, full-blooded, to quiet, by sheer will power and a turn of thought. The force of mastery was strong in Black Dennis Nolan's wild nature. When he wished it he could master himself as well as others. Now he sat down quietly beside his fire and lit his pipe. The evening was near at hand – the evening of the third and last day of his exile. The sun, like a small round window of red glass, hung low above the black hills to the north and west. He got to his feet, threw snow on the breaking fire and scattered the steaming coals with his foot. Then he pulled down his shelter and threw the poles and spruce branches into a thicket, so that no marks of his encampment were left except the wet coals and smudged ashes of the fire.

The crimson sun slid down out of sight behind the black hills to the west and north, and the gray twilight thickened over the wilderness. The last red tint had faded from the west and the windows of the cabins were glowing when the skipper reached the top of the path leading down to Chance Along. A dog barked – Pat Kavanagh's black crackie – and the whisper of the tide fumbling at edges of ice came up from the land-wash below the fish-house and drying-stages. He saw the spars of his little schooner etched black against the slate-gray of the eastern sky. He stood at the edge of the broken slope, looking and listening. Presently he heard a mutter of voices and saw two dark figures ascending the path.

"Good evenin', men," he said.

The two halted. "Glory be!" exclaimed the voice of Bill Brennen. "The skipper himself, sure, praise the saints! Bes it yerself, skipper, an' no mistake?"

"Aye, Bill, an' why for not?" returned Nolan. "Didn't ye t'ink as I could make the trip to Witless Bay an' back in t'ree days? Bes that yerself, Nick Leary?"

"Aye, skipper, aye," replied Nick. The two were now at the top of the path, staring anxiously at the skipper through the gloom. Leary's head was still in a bandage.

"We was jist a-settin' out to look for ye, skipper," said Bill.

Black Dennis Nolan laughed at that. "Was ye t'inkin' I

couldn't find me way back to me own harbor, in fair weather?" he asked.

"Aye, skipper, sure ye could," said Bill Brennen; "but it bes like this wid us. Dick Lynch give us the slip this very day, wid a bottle o' rum in his belly an' the smoke of it in his head, an' a gun in his hand. Aye, skipper, an' we didn't larn it till only a minute ago from little Patsy Burke."

"Aye, that bes the right o' it," broke in Nick Leary. "We heard tell o' Dick Lynch a-slippin' away to the south'ard jist this minute from little Patsy Burke. Drunk as a bo's'un he was, wid his old swilin'-gun on his shoulder an' the divil's own flare in the eyes o' him. So we hauled out too, skipper, intendin' to catch him afore he come up wid yerself if the saints would give us the luck."

"Sure, then, I didn't catch a sight o' the treacherous squid," said the skipper. "Ye see, b'ys, I took a swing off to the westward to-day to spy out some timber. But what would Dick Lynch be huntin' me wid his swilin'-gun for? Why for d'ye say he was huntin' me? Didn't I put the comather on to him last time? The divil's own courage must be in him if he bes out huntin' for me."

"He was tryin' all he knowed how to raise trouble yesterday," said Bill; "but the b'ys wasn't wid him. This very mornin', when I called in to see how he was feelin' for work, there he laid in his bed wid the covers drug up over his ugly face, a-moanin' an' groanin' as how he wasn't fit to hit a clip. Then we all o' us goes off to the choppin', to cut timber for his riverence's blessed little church, an' mugs-up in the woods widout comin' home, an' when we gets back to the harbor, maybe a few minutes afore sundown, little Patsy Burke gives us the word as how Dick Lynch went off wid a gun, swearin' by the whole assembly of heaven as how he'd be blowin' yer heart out o' ye the minute he clapped eye on ye. An' then, skipper dear, Pat Kavanagh's girl Mary comes a-runnin' wid word as how Dick Lynch t'iefed a bottle o' rum from Pat himself and was brow-sprit under wid the glory of it an' fit to take a shot – except for the aim of him – at Saint Peter himself. She telled as how he'd shaped his course to the south'ard, with his gun on his shoulder, swearin' he'd blow the head off ye or never come home to Chance Along no more. So Nick an' me puts two an' two forninst each other an' figgered as how Dick would have ye if somethin' didn't happen to t'row out his plans."

"Ye bain't got the right o' it there, Bill," said Nick. " 'Twas Mary told us to follow after Dick Lynch. She'd gone herself, she said, but she'd heard o' it no more'n a minute ago from Pat, her bein' over to the skipper's house an' tryin' to cheer up the lady what come off the wrack! 'Save the skipper,' says Mary, the eyes o' her like lumps o' ice on the coast in June. 'Save him from the drunk dog wid the gun, even if it bes the death o' yerselves.' Aye, that bes what Mary Kavanagh said to us – an' here we bes, skipper."

"Mary bes a good girl," said the skipper. Then he laughed harshly and slapped Bill Brennen on the back.

"Me brains bes still in me head an' me hands on the ends o' me two arms," he exclaimed; "but what bes happenin' to Dick Lynch, I wonder? If ever he comes back – but he'll not dare! Aye, ye kin lay to that. He'd as soon jump into hell wid the divil as come back now to Chance Along. Maybe he'll be losin' himself like Foxey Jack Quinn went an' done wid himself. Aye, lads, fools kin tell as how me luck bes gone – but the saints themselves bes wid me, drivin' me enemies out o' Chance Along widout me so much as havin' to kill one o' them!"

"Sure, skipper, it looks that way, an' no mistake," said Bill Brennen. "The saints be wid ye for the kind heart ye has for helpless women an' childer, an' for yer love o' Father McQueen, an' for the work ye bes at to build the little church; but most of all, skipper, for the kind heart o' ye to every helpless woman an' child."

A scowl, or was it a shadow, crossed Black Dennis Nolan's face at that.

"Sure, a kind heart bes a grand t'ing," he said, – "and so bes sharp wits an' hard hands!"

They turned and went down the path. Mother Nolan met the skipper just inside the door, with the big wooden spoon from the stew-pot dripping in her hand. Her black eyes looked blacker and keener than usual as they met those of her grandson.

"So here ye be, safe back from Witless Bay," she said. "Ye didn't waste a minute, Denny."

"Sure I didn't," returned the skipper, quickly. "It beed fair weather an' fair goin' all the way an' one little letter bain't much o' a pack to tote. How be ye all, Granny? How bes the lass from the wrack?"

"Grand altogether," said the old woman, returning to the stove and the pot of stew.

"Aye," said young Cormick, "she was singin' to-day fit to drag the heart o' ye out t'rough yer ears. Sure, Denny, if ye heard a fairy singin' 'twould sound no grander!"

"Aye, like a fairy," agreed the old woman, wagging her head. "I bain't wonderin' a mite at how she brought the salt tears a-hoppin' out o' the eyes o' the blessed Queen herself! An' she was that happy, Denny, a-t'inkin' o' how her letter to up-along was safe an' sure on its way, that didn't she have Pat Kavanagh down wid his fiddle, an' atween the two o' 'em they made the finest music was ever heard on this coast. Her heart bes fair set on up-along, Denny, an' on what she calls her career, meanin' songs an' glory an' money an' her name on the lips o' men."

The skipper was silent for a moment after that, staring at the floor. He raised his eyes to the old woman and found that she was gazing at him fixedly.

"Sure, an' why for not?" he said. "An' what bes she doin' now?"

"Sleepin'," replied Mother Nolan. "Sleepin' an' dreamin' o' up-along an' all her grand friends."

A scowl darkened the skipper's eyes and brow, but he had no remark to make on the matter of the lady's dreams. He threw aside his outer coat, ate his supper, smoked his pipe, and at last retired to his bed. In the meantime, Nick Leary had taken word to Pat and Mary Kavanagh that the skipper was home in Chance Along, safe and sound, having missed Dick Lynch by shaping his course westward to spy out timber. Mary's face brightened at the news. Pat glanced at her, then nodded his tangled head toward Leary.

"The skipper bes still alive an' the letter bes gone on its way," he said. "So, come spring, they be takin' that singin' lady wid the eyes o' magic away from Chance Along. Maybe they'll be comin' for her widout waitin' for spring? She bes a wonder at the singin', an' no mistake – the best I ever hear in all me v'yages into foreign ports. An' the looks o' her! Holy saints, they bain't scarce human!"

Nick Leary grinned through his bandage.

"Aye, Pat, ye've got the discarnin' eye in yer head – ye an' the skipper," he said. "However the skipper kep' himself away from Chance Along for t'ree entire days, wid herself a-singin' an' a-flashin' her eyes right in his own house, bes a puzzle to me. Aye, sure it do, for didn't I see her put the spell o' women on him the very first minute she opened her eyes at him on the fore-top o' the wrack."

"Leave the skipper be, Nick Leary," said Mary. "Never half a word would ye be sayin' if he could hear ye. Leave him an' his business be. He bes a good friend to ye – aye, an' to every soul in the harbour who don't cross him."

"Sure, Mary, I bain't meanin' naught," returned Nick. "Sure he bes a good friend to me!"

Pat Kavanagh smiled and took up his fiddle and his bow. His hands were still for a minute, and then the instrument began to sigh and trill. The sounds gathered in strength, soared high, then thinned and sank to no more than the whisper of a tune – and then Pat began to sing. This is part of what he sang :–

Come all ye hardy fishermen
An' harken to me song,
O' how the mermaid from the wrack
Come ashore in Chance Along.

Her eyes was like the sea in June,
Her lips was like a rose,
Her voice was like a fairy bell
A-ringin' crost the snows.

The Skipper he forgot the wrack,
Forgot the waves a-rollin',
For she had put the witchy spell
On Skipper Dennis Nolan.

. . . . . .

Come all ye hardy fishermen
An' larn from this me song,
To turn yer eyes the other way
To the girls from up-along.

"Yer songs get more foolish every day, father dear," said Mary.

"Sure, Pat, Mary bes right," said Leary. "Ye sings as if the girls in Chance Along hadn't so much as one eye in the heads o' the entire crew o' them. Now I bes t'inkin' as how there bes a girl in this harbor wid eyes an' lips –"

"Sure, Nick, yer thoughts bes no better nor father's songs," interrupted Mary.

BLACK DENNIS NOLAN was permitted an interview with Miss Flora Lockhart in the afternoon following his return to Chance Along. The singer was sitting up in a chair by the fire, wrapped about in her own silk dressing-gown, which had been brought ashore from the wreck, and in an eiderdown quilt. Her plentiful, soft, brown hair was arranged in a manner new to Chance Along, and stuck through with a wonderful comb of amber shell and gold, and a pin with a jewelled hilt. The ornaments for the hair had been supplied by Mother Nolan, who had possessed them for the past thirty years, hidden away in the bottom of a nunney-bag. Her own son, the late skipper, had salvaged them from a wreck. Flora had her own rings on her tapering fingers. There was color in her flawless cheeks, her wonderful eyes were bright and clear, and her lips were red. She smiled at the skipper when Mother Nolan ushered him into the room.

"It was very, very kind of you to take my letter all the way to the post-office with your own hand," she said. Her bell-like voice was generous and sincere. "I wish I could reward you for all you have done for me, Mr. Nolan. But how can I – except in my heart? You are so rich and proud, I am afraid to offer you money." Here there was a playful note in her voice which the skipper detected. So she was making fun of his wealth and his pride. His dark face flushed with several disturbing emotions. To be addressed by the title of "mister" added to his discomfort. There were no misters in Chance Along – or anywhere on the coast, except the Methodist preacher in Bay Bulls, away to the north. He was skipper – or just Denny Nolan. He was skipper of Chance Along – not a preacher and not the mate of a foreign-going ship.

"Sure, it bain't no great trip to Witless Bay an' back agin," he mumbled, staring at the girl in the big chair. The light that entered the room from the gray afternoon, by way of the small window, was more of a shadow than an illumination. The red fire in the wide chimney warmed a little of it, painted the low ceiling and touched the girl's eyes with a sunset tint. The skipper shuffled his feet on a rag mat and crumpled his cap between his big hands. He felt like a slave – aye, and something of a rogue – here in his own house. But he tried to brace himself with the thought that he was master of the situation.

"Please sit down and talk to me, Mr. Nolan," said Flora.

The skipper glanced around the room. Mother Nolan had gone, leaving the door ajar behind her. A small wooden stool stood near the fire, directly across it from Flora. The skipper advanced to the stool and sat down, the thumping of his heart sounding in his ears like the strokes of a sledgehammer on wood. For a moment the sight of his strong eyes was veiled by a mist – by an inner mist smoking up from the heat and commotion of his blood. When his sight cleared he saw the beautiful young woman regarding him with a slight smile on her red lips and in her wonderful eyes. There was inquiry in the smile – yes, and pity and amusement were in it, too. The young man felt short of breath and at the same time a choking sensation as of uncomfortable fulness of the lungs. He stared across at her like one spellbound. The girl's glance wavered, but her smile deepened. A brief note of laughter, like a chime of glass bells, parted her lips.

"Dear me, you look very tragic," she said. "You look as if you saw a ghost."

The skipper started violently and turned his face to the fire. He laughed huskily, then got to his feet and looked down at her with the firelight red as blood in his black eyes. Suddenly he groaned, stooped and snatched up one of her white, bejewelled hands. He pressed it passionately to his lips, crushing the delicate fingers with his. For a second or two the singer was far too amazed and horrified to speak or act; then, recovering suddenly, she wrenched her hand free and struck him on the cheek. He flung his head back and stood straight. A short, thin, red line showed beneath his right eye where a diamond in one of her rings had scratched the skin.

"How dare you?" she cried, her voice trembling and her face colorless. "Go away! You forget – who I am! You are a coward!"

The skipper did not flinch, his eyes did not waver. She was but a woman, after all, for all her talk of queens and fame. He had kissed her hand – and she had struck him. Well? He was rich. He would marry her – and she would soon learn to love him. He looked down at her with a smile on his lips and the light of mastery in his black eyes.

"Go away – you coward!" she cried. Then she hid her face in her hands and began to sob. Tears glinted between her fingers, beside the diamonds. At that moment Mother Nolan entered and clutched her grandson by the elbow.

"Get out wid ye, ye great hulkin' fool!" she exclaimed. "Oh, I seed ye a-clawin' at her little hand. An' now ye've set her to weepin', ye great lump! Bain't there a drop o' wits in yer head? Don't ye know yer place, Denny Nolan, ye ignorant fisherman, a-pawin' at the likes o' her?"

The skipper felt shame at sight of Flora's tears and anger at his grandmother's humiliating words. There was a bitter edge to her voice that was new to him, and her lean old fingers pinched into his flesh like fingers of iron.

"Sure, I bes mad," he said. " 'Twas only a trick, anyhow – an' I did no harm. There bain't naught for ye to be cryin' about."

He strode from the room, with old Mother Nolan still clinging to his elbow. When they reached the kitchen she loosed her clutch on his elbow.

"Denny Nolan, ye bes a fool!" she exclaimed. "Saints presarve us, Denny, what would ye be doin' wid a sprite the like o' her, wid a heart all full entirely o' gold an' diamonds an' queens an' kings? – an' girls in this very harbor, ye great ninney, wid red woman hearts in their breasts!"

The skipper stared at her for a second, muttered an oath, crushed his fur cap on his head and went out into the gray twilight, slamming the door behind him. He blundered his way up the path at the back of the harbor and held on, blindly, to the westward.

"Sure, now she'll be frightened o' me all the time," he muttered. "I was a fool to fright her so! Maybe now she'll never be marryin' wid me at all. The divil was into me! Aye, the divil himself!"

He came presently to a group of his men working in a belt of timber, and this encounter brought him back to affairs of the common day. Grabbing an axe from young Peter Leary, he set to with a fury of effort and unheeding skill that brought the slim spruces flapping to earth. Men had to jump to save themselves from being crushed. The white chips flew in the gray twilight; and Bill Brennen wondered what imp's claw had marked the skipper under the eyes and crisscrossed his temper.

The weather continued cold, cloudless and windless through-out the next three days. During that time the skipper made no effort to see Flora, but was abroad from sun-up to sun-down with the men, cutting out timber for the little church as if his life depended on it. No sight or sound of Dick Lynch came back to the harbor. This gave Bill Brennen an argument in favor of loyalty to the skipper. He preached it to the men, and it made a great impression on their simple though dangerous natures.

"There was Foxey Jack Quinn," he said. "Jack hated the skipper like we hates sea-water in our rum. Didn't he try to kill him – t'row him over the cliff – an' didn't the skipper put the comather on to him? An' then he ups an' busts into the skipper's house, wid the intention o' t'iefing the money – an' where bes Foxey Jack Quinn this minute? The saints only knows! – or maybe the divil could tell ye! An' there was Dick Lynch. Dick ups an' crosses the skipper in the store, an' gets his head broke. Nex', he raises a mutiny agin the skipper an' slips his knife into a mate. Nex', he fills himself up wid rum an' sets out wid his swilin'-gun to blow the skipper's head away! An' where bes Dick Lynch this minute? Aye, where bes he! Tell me that, if ye kin – I don't know, an' ye don't know, an' the skipper himself don't know. But the saints knows! – or maybe it bes the divil himself could tell ye! Anyhow, all the luck o' this harbor bes wid the skipper an' wid them as stands true wid him. Aye, ye kin lay to that! His enemies blink out like a spark floatin' up in the air. B'ys, stick wid the skipper! He feeds ye like marchants. Already every man o' ye has more gold stored away nor ye ever see afore in all yer life, an' come spring the skipper'll be freightin' yer jewels, an' the cargo out o' the last wrack, north to St. John's, an' sellin' 'em for ye. Would ye have salved 'em widout the skipper? No. Would ye be able for to freight 'em to St. John's widout himself an' his fore-an'-after? No. An' neither would ye be able to sell 'em even if ye could freight 'em! Stand true to Black Dennis Nolan, b'ys, an' ye'll all be fat an' rich as marchants, wid never the need to wet a line at the fishin'."

Dick Lynch had gone away drunk; but not so drunk as to have forgotten to take food and a blanket with him, and to stow away on his person his share of the gold from the *Durham Castle*. His inflamed mind must have held a doubt as to the certainty of meeting and disposing of the skipper.

After the long spell of fine weather another "flurry" swirled out of the west, and sent the men of Chance Along into their cabins, to eat and drink and spin yarns and keep the fires roaring in the little, round stoves and blackened chimneys. Throughout the first day of storm the skipper sat by the stove in his kitchen, talking pleasantly enough to Mother Nolan and Cormick, figuring on the plans for the church which Father McQueen had left with him, but with never a question about Flora Lockhart. He was something of a dissembler, was the skipper – when his blood was cool. Mother Nolan spoke once of the girl, saying that the loneliness of Chance Along was eating her poor heart; but the skipper gave no heed to it. On the morning of the second day of the storm, after Mother Nolan had carried tea, bacon and toast to the singer and was eating her own breakfast with her grandsons, the inner door opened and Flora herself entered the kitchen. The three looked up at her in amazement. The skipper was the first to lower his eyes.

"Good mornin' to ye," he said, and went on with his breakfast.

"Oh, I am so dull and lonely," exclaimed the girl. "This terrible storm frightens me. Why must I stay in that dreary room all by myself?"

"Ye be welcome to the entire house, ye poor dear," said Mother Nolan. "But has ye et yer breakfast?"

"Not yet. The storm howled so in the chimney that I was too frightened to eat. Mayn't I bring it out here and eat it with you – and listen to you talking?" begged Flora.

"Sure ye kin. Set right down an' I'll fetch yer tray," said Mother Nolan.

"Aye, that ye kin – an' welcome ye be as June," said the skipper quietly.

The singer glanced at him shyly, uncertainly, with a question in her beautiful eyes.

"You are very kind – you are all very kind," she said. "I fear that I was very – rude to you, Mr. Nolan. I – I struck you – but you were rough. And I – called you names – which I did not mean."

"Let it pass," said the skipper, gazing at the bacon on his plate. "I bes rough, as ye say. It bes the way I was born an' bred. But I was meanin' no disrespect to ye, as the holy saints be me jedges. Sure I – I couldn't help meself!"

So it happened that Miss Flora Lockhart ate her breakfast

beside the kitchen stove with Mother Nolan, the skipper and young Cormick. The way she ate was a wonder to watch, all so easy and quiet and polite. Mother Nolan wagged her head over it, as much as to say that such table manners would bring no good to such a place as Chance Along, and young Cormick could do nothing but stare at the beautiful stranger. She talked brightly, with the evident intention to please. It was her nature to want to impress people favorably toward her – and after all, she owed a great deal to these people and, for a few weeks longer at least, was entirely in their power. She saw that the skipper was a strong man – a man to be feared – and that her charms had ensnared his wild heart. Therefore she must play the game artfully with him instead of continuing the crude and honest method of slaps in the face. She believed that he would prove harmless and docile if skilfully handled, but as dangerous as a wounded animal if insulted and rebuffed.

After breakfast she asked for Pat Kavanagh. She did not remember his name, but spoke of him as the funny old fellow with the violin and the wooden leg.

"If he were here we could have a fine concert," she said, "and forget all about the terrible wind and snow whirling around the house." Her laughing face was turned to the skipper.

"Sure then, Pat bes the lad we wants," said the skipper, grinning like one entranced by a glimpse of heaven itself. There was a golden vision in his head, poor fool, of this beautiful creature sitting beneath his roof for all time, her red lips and wonderful eyes always laughing at him, her silvery voice forever telling him to forget the storm outside. The future looked to him like a state of bliss such as one sometimes half-sees, half-feels, in dreams.

"I'll go fetch him an' his fiddle," he said, pulling on his heavy jumper.

"Now don't ye be losin' yerself in the flurry," continued Mother Nolan.

"It bes nought, Granny," returned the skipper. "Sure I kin feel me way on me hands an' knees."

It took him fifteen minutes to find Pat Kavanagh's shanty and locate the door of it, so blinding and choking was the storm. He pushed the door open, stumbled into the warmth, and slammed the timbers shut behind him. Mary was sewing beside the stove, and Pat was mumbling over the first verse of a new "come-all-ye." They looked up at the skipper in astonishment.

"What the divil bes troublin' ye, Denny Nolan, to fetch ye out o' yer own house sich a day as this?" demanded the ex-sailorman. "Bes there anything the matter wid that grand young lady from up-along?"

The skipper removed his cap and with it beat the snow from his limbs and body. He breathed heavily from his struggle with the storm. Mary eyed him anxiously, her hands idle in her lap.

"I's come to fetch yer over to me own house — ye an' yer fiddle," said Nolan.

"The divil ye has!" retorted Pat Kavanagh. "Saints presarve ye, lad, what kind o' rum has ye bin a-drinkin' of this mornin' already?"

"Herself bes wantin' ye, Pat — ye an' yer fiddle, for to have a concert wid," said the skipper, with childlike trust and delight in his voice.

"Skipper, dear, would ye be haulin' me an' me wooden leg out into sich a desperate flurry as this here?" inquired Pat, aghast. "Saints be good to ye, skipper, but I'd die in me tracks!"

Some of the foolish delight went out of Nolan's face. His lips closed and his black eyes began to glint like moonshine on new ice.

"It bain't no more nor a step or two," he said. "If ye can't walk it yerself, Pat, — ye an' yer wooden leg, — then I kin tote ye on me back."

"Sure ye kin go, father; an' I'll be goin' along wid the two o' ye," said Mary. "The poor lass bes wantin' amusement, an' it be but right for us all to give it her. Music an' a concert she bes wantin' to keep up her poor little heart agin the storm. Sure, an' why not? Did ye think for her — a slip o' a grand concert-singer from up-along — to have a heart for the wind an' snows o' Chance Along?"

Pat grumbled. The skipper looked at Mary.

"There bain't nothin' wrong wid her heart," he said.

"Sure there bain't," agreed Mary. "Her poor little heart bes jist sick to death o' Chance Along — an' what else would ye look for? Sprees an' company she must be havin', day after day, an' night after night, like what she has always had. It bes our duty to amuse her, father, an' feed her an' nurse her, till her grand folks up-along takes her away."

The skipper was not altogether satisfied with Mary's words. They did not seem to voice his own ideas on the subject at all, though they were evidently intended to agree with his attitude toward the singer. They had a back-snap to them that he mistrusted.

Half an hour later all three were safe in the skipper's kitchen, breathless and coated with snow. Flora welcomed Mary with a kiss.

"What a beauty you are," she exclaimed.

Mary's rosy cheeks deepened in color at the praise, and a shadow came out from the depths of her gray eyes. Mother Nolan saw all this, though she seemed to be very busy with getting poor Pat and his wooden leg into a chair.

Well, a punch was brewed, and Pat played on his fiddle, and Flora Lockhart sang as no one but herself ever sang before on that coast — yes, or anywhere else in the whole island of Newfoundland. The wonder of her singing even set young Cormick's heart to aching with nameless and undreamed of aches. As for the skipper, he looked as if the fairies had caught him for sure!

IN CHANCE ALONG the wintry days and weeks crawled by, with cold and thaw, wind, snow and fog. Flora Lockhart waited in vain for a reply to her letter. At last her suspicions were awakened by a word from Mother Nolan; so she wrote another letter and gave it to the old woman. The old woman gave it to Mary Kavanagh, and Mary in turn put it into the hands of one of the young men of the harbor, with instructions to take it to Witless Bay and from there send it out by mail. The young man promised to do all this, of course.

"An' mind ye," cautioned Mary, "don't ye go an' let the skipper know what ye bes up to."

Now this young man was one of the dozen who wanted Mary Kavanagh for a wife. He was not brave, he was not honest; but he was as cunning as a fox. So he thought the matter over, and soon came to the conclusion that the game was not worth the candle. He was afraid of the skipper; and he was content that the girl from up-along should remain in the harbor and continue to blind the skipper's heart to the charms of Mary Kavanagh. So he went quietly to the master, put the letter in his hands and told him what he knew of it. Dennis Nolan destroyed the letter, and told the young man to keep himself out of sight for the next three days. The infatuated skipper had not yet given up hope of winning the heart of the wonderful creature from up-along.

Late in March a French brig, bound for St. Pierre, went ashore on the Squid Rocks to the north of Chance Along. Only two of her crew reached the land-wash alive. They were powerful fellows, swarthy as Arabs, with gold rings in their ears, the devil in their hearts, and a smattering of many languages on their tongues. The gale that had driven the brig on the Squid Rocks had interrupted them in the hatching of a mutiny against their captain, mate and boatswain; for the brig's cargo consisted of silks and wines for the smugglers of St. Pierre, and two chests of gold containing the half-year's pay of the Governor, officials, and soldiers of the little island.

Black Dennis Nolan and his men found them on the landwash, more dead than alive, dragged them back out of reach of the spray, and laid them on blankets beside a fire. The brig was well in among the rocks, going to pieces fast. After two hours of daring effort the skipper and four of his men reached her, and found the chests of French gold in the lazaret beneath the captain's cabin. They remained aboard the wreck for nearly an hour before venturing shoreward with the treasure. They salvaged the chests at last, however, placed a guard over them, and made one more trip to the brig and back, bringing a bale or two of silk and a cask of red wine the second time. Then the brig melted and fell to pieces before their eyes. It was not until then that any one noticed that the two swarthy sailors had recovered and departed, taking with them the blankets and bottle of rum which had been employed in reviving them. The skipper swore mightily at this discovery, knocked a few of his men about, then had the chests of gold stowed on two handsleds and set out for home in full force and at top speed. On reaching Chance Along he learned that the two swarthy strangers had already been there, and departed with two sealing-guns and a bag of food. The skipper sent Bill Brennen and six men on their tracks, for he did not want the strangers to carry out to the world the news of the wreck of the brig and the salving of the treasure-chests. He did not follow them himself because the chests had to be opened, and their contents divided and hidden away immediately, and the chests themselves destroyed.

The gold was divided into forty equal parts. One part was given, or laid aside, for every man who had been to the Squid Rocks; two parts went to each of the men who had accompanied the skipper to the brig itself, and four were kept by the skipper. There was no grumbling this time. The harvest was rich beyond the wildest dream and had been fairly shared. The money belonging to the men who had gone after the two strangers was placed in the hands of sons, wives or fathers.

"Hide it away, men," said the skipper, "for if them two pirates gets clear away, they'll sure be back some day wid a crew o' blackguards like themselves, to try to t'ief all our property away from us."

Bill Brennen and his party returned before sundown, carrying a wounded comrade and a dead Frenchman along with them. There had been an ambush and a fight, and one of the sailors had escaped clean away. The skipper was in a rage; but, as the faithful Bill Brennen had commanded the party and Nick Leary had been a member of it, he kept his hands and feet still and let nothing fly but curses.

Now we must look around for Dick Lynch, who did not go out of this history when he departed so boldly from Chance Along with his sealing-gun on his shoulder. Far from it. Dick was intended for greater things than he knew.

A week after the wreck of the French brig on the Squid Rocks, Dick Lynch entered a public-house situated near the eastern end of Water Street, St. John's, sat down at a table near the fire and called for rum. Though Dick consumed much rum, he did not often buy it at this establishment; for he roomed in Mother McKay's cottage on the hill, back of the city, and Mother McKay kept a shebeen. To-day, however, Dick had felt that he could stand no more of Mother McKay's liquor nor of the honest dame's society, either. The rum was weak and harsh and the society was distracting to his thoughts. What he wanted was matured liquor and quiet, so that he might nail down his somewhat vague plans of returning to Chance Along and overthrowing the skipper thereof. The hour was that of the evening dusk. He was alone in this particular room of the *Ship Ahoy Hotel*, but he could hear the voices of other imbibers barking and rolling from an adjoining apartment. He gulped down half of his rum and lit his pipe. The proprietor entered then, threw a lump of coal on the fire and lit a ship's lantern that hung from the middle rafter. Next moment, the outer door opened, and a man entered from the muddy street, his sou'easter, oilskin coat and ruddy young face all agleam with moisture.

"Good evenin' to ye, Mister Darlin'," said the proprietor. "Foul weather, bain't it, sir?"

"Aye, Jake, foul weather it is," returned the young man, throwing aside his dripping hat. "Bring me whiskey, – hot, with a slice of lemon in it and a lump of sugar."

Jake departed, and Mr. Darling sat down beside the fire and pulled a short wooden pipe from an inner pocket. In repose, his young, clean-shaven face wore an expression of gravity that verged upon the dismal. He filled his pipe with cut tobacco from a leather bag, lit it and then glanced at Dick Lynch through a puff of twisting blue smoke. He caught Dick's eyes full upon him, for that worthy had been staring at him ever since he had removed his dripping sou'easter. He removed his pipe from his mouth and leaned forward.

"Hullo!" he said. "I'll swear this isn't the first time I've seen that black mug of yours, my man! But it wasn't in St. John's — an' it wasn't aboard any ship."

Dick Lynch was of the same way of thinking, for he recognized this young man as the officer from the *Durham Castle*, who had commanded the party that had been left behind by Captain McTavish to guard the wreck of that good ship. He took another swig at his glass and shifted his eyes to the fire.

"Sure, sir, ye may be right," he said. "Was it in Harbor Grace ye seed me?"

"No. I have never set foot in Harbor Grace," returned Mr. Darling.

"That bes my home, sir — Harbor Grace," lied Dick, cheerfully.

Just then Jake entered with Mr. Darling's toddy. He set it at the young sailor's elbow, hoped it was entirely to his taste, and retired. Darling sipped the toddy, puffed twice at his pipe, then fixed his keen glance upon Lynch's face.

"Don't lie to me," he said. "Your mug is too ugly to forget easy! You are the big, cussing pirate the savages gave the name of skipper to, along on that devilish coast to the south where we lost the *Durham Castle*. You are a sly fellow, and a daring one; but it will not help you a mite to sit there and talk about your happy home in Harbor Grace to me."

"The skipper!" exclaimed Dick Lynch, in genuine anger and dismay. "Saints presarve ye, I'd as soon be took for the divil himself as for Black Dennis Nolan o' Chance Along. No, sir, I bain't that tyrant, though some folks do say as how I bes about his size and color."

"Is that so?" enquired Mr. Darling, quietly. "You are not the skipper of Chance Along, but you look like him. Is that the way of it?"

"Aye, that bes the way of it, sir."

"You know this skipper fellow, then?"

"Aye, sir, to me cost — may the divil fly away wid him! Hasn't he bullied me an' cheated me all me life long, the divil-possessed tyrant! Bain't he the livin' curse o' Chance Along?"

"Chance Along, is it?" murmured Mr. Darling. "Now where the devil is Chance Along?"

Then, raising his voice, "You don't seem to love this skipper fellow — this Black Dennis Nolan. What is the trouble between the pair of you?"

Dick finished his rum, eyed the other suspiciously, then stared sullenly at the fire.

Mr. Darling smiled grimly and shouted for Jake.

"My friend will have more of the same," he said, pointing to Lynch's empty glass. "But make it hot, Jake. This is no kind of weather for cold liquor. Better bring the bottle right along, and the kettle and sugar too."

Twenty minutes later Dick Lynch began to talk again, his belated caution entirely vaporized and blown out of his somewhat inferior brain by the fumes of hot rum, lemon and sugar.

"I knows ye, sir," he said. "Sure, didn't I know ye the minute I clapped me two eyes on ye. Cap'n o' that big ship that came ashore in Nolan's Cove, t'ree miles to the south o' Chance Along, ye be. An' a smart landin' ye made, too, boat by boat, wid every mother's son o' ye wid a gun an' a sword in his two hands. Sure, sir, ye wasn't lookin' for to meet wid no man-killin' wrackers on *that* coast, was ye? Saints forgive ye, the babe unborn would be safe to come ashore in Chance Along!"

John Darling smiled. "You are a sharp lad," he said. "I saw it in your eyes that you knew me the moment I entered the room. I don't see how I ever came to mistake a smart, well-spoken lad like you for that fellow you call the skipper. Well, I am sorry for it. But you have made one mistake, my lad. I wasn't the captain of that ship. I was only one of the mates."

"Well, sir," returned Lynch, cordially, "I bain't sharp enough for to see much difference atween a cap'n an' a mate. Ye looks like a cap'n to me, anyhow."

He paused, poured more rum and hot water, sampled the brew and continued.

"Now I feels it a shame, sir, the way Black Dennis Nolan made a fool o' the lot o' ye, wid his lies about Frenchman's Cove an' Nap Harbor. Sure, I felt desperate bad about it at the time – an' now I feels worse. Aye, sir, worse, seein' as how ye be sich a fine, grand ginerous young gintleman as ye be. An' then the way he ups an' takes all yer gold an' fine jewels away from ye, an' ye t'inkin' all the time 'twas the folk o' Nap Harbor done it!"

"Yes, it was certainly an unmannerly trick," said Darling, quietly. "I suppose he took it all to Chance Along – gold, jewels and everything – and kept it for himself?"

"He kep' more nor his share o' the sovereigns, ye kin lay to that, sir; an' as for the rings an' sich fancy trinkets – well, sir, he says as how we'll all be gettin' our share come June an' he gets 'round to St. John's here to sell 'em. But there bain't no share for me, sir. I fit for me rights, I did – an' here I be!"

The interview continued for another hour, and during the glowing, rum-inspired course of it, Dick Lynch told all that he knew of Chance Along, its manners, its skipper and its exact location. He confessed that he had never seen a great diamond and ruby necklace, but that he had seen a whole casket full of jewels and was willing to swear by all the saints aloft that the casket was still in Chance Along. He did not notice that Mr. Darling was spending all his time over one small glass of whiskey toddy. Finding the young officer a good listener and an agreeable companion, he went on to tell of the wreck of the *Royal William*, of the panic in the flooded cabin, and at last of the beautiful young woman with the voice like fairy bells and eyes like a mermaid's eyes.

Mr. Darling sat up at that and laid his pipe on the table.

"A full-rigged ship, you say? What was her name?" he asked, anxiously.

"The name o' the ship? Well, sir, far's I kin remember it was the *Rile Willyum*. Aye, sir that was it."

Mr. Darling got excited. His face went dead white, then flaming red, and he leaned forward and gripped the fingers of his right hand in Lynch's shoulder. But Dick was too mellow and happy to object or to feel surprise.

"And what was the lady's name?" cried Mr. Darling. "Out with it, man! Out with it! What was *her* name?"

"Name o' the lady? Lady's name? Her name? Sure, sir, it bes Nora."

"Nora! Don't you mean Flora?"

"Aye, Flora. Sure, sir, Flora bes what I said."

"God!" exclaimed Mr. Darling, leaning back in his chair. Dick Lynch smiled across at him. He recovered himself in a minute.

"With a beautiful voice, you say?" he queried faintly.

"Aye, sir. Sure, didn't she sing a song afore the Queen herself," returned Dick.

"It is Flora!" cried the other. "My God, it is Flora!" Then gripping Lynch again, "Did you say – did you say she – she is – well?" he whispered.

"Sure, I told ye she bes well," replied the befuddled fisherman. "Well, d'ye say? Aye, she bes plump as a pa'tridge, a-livin' on the fat o' the land – the fat o' all the wracks that comes up from the sea. An' a beauty she bes, altogether. Saints presarve ye, sir, she bes the beautifulest female woman ever come ashore on that coast. She was desperate bad wid the fever, was Nora, when first the skipper took her home wid him; but now she bes plump as a young swile, sir, an' too beautiful entirely for the likes o' meself to look at."

Mr. Darling's face went white again.

"The skipper?" he asked, huskily. "For God's sake, man, what are you saying? Why does she stay in Chance Along? What has she to do with that damned big black beast you call the skipper?"

"Now you bes a-gettin' excited, sir, all along o' that Nora girl," protested Dick Lynch. "She bes a-livin' wid Mother Nolan, in the skipper's own house. The skipper bes figgerin' on coaxin' of her 'round to marry wid him; but I hears, sir, as how she told him as how she'd marry no poor, ignorant, dacent fisherman at all, but a king wid a golden crown on his head. Aye, sir, that bes the trut'. The likes o' she be well able to keep Black Denny Nolan in his place."

"Thank God!" exclaimed Mr. Darling, sitting back in his chair again.

Dick Lynch eyed him with drunken cunning.

"Ye knows that grand young woman, sir?" he queried.

"Yes," said Mr. Darling. "She crossed to London aboard my ship three years ago. We – we were good friends."

"Aye, ye would be," returned Dick with a drunken leer. And then, lurching forward, "Ye'll be makin' a trip 'round to Chance Along I bes t'inkin', sir, to put the comather on to this Dennis Nolan? Sure, an' why not? The dirty squid bes as full o' gold an' riches as any marchant. I'll be goin' along wid ye, sir – if ye gives me two pistols an' takes two yerself. I'll show ye where the harbor bes, an' his own house wid Nora in it – an' all. If we gets to the harbor quiet, about the middle o' the night, we'll shoot the skipper in his bed, the black divil, afore he kin so much as lay a curse on to us. I bes wid ye, sir. Ye kin trust Dick Lynch as ye would yer own mother."

Mr. Darling said that he had a great deal of business to attend to in the city, but that he would meet Dick Lynch in this very room, at nine o'clock in the morning, five days later. He did not mean a word of it, for he would not have trusted that worthy any farther than he could have thrown him over his shoulder. But he arranged the meeting and promised to supply plenty of pistols for the expedition. Then he said good night and went out of the warm room and fumes of rum to the mud and driving sleet of the night, leaving Dick Lynch smiling to himself at thought of what his enemy, the skipper, would say when he woke up in bed some fine morning and found himself dead.

XV ❦ *Mr. Darling Sets Out on a Journey*

THIS JOHN DARLING was no ordinary shell-back. His father was an English parson, his uncle a Fellow of Wadham College, Oxford, and his eldest brother a commander in the Royal Navy. John was poor in worldly gear, however, and had recently been third officer of the *Durham Castle*. Now he was without a berth, and was making a bid for fortune of an unusual and adventurous kind. In London, Sir Ralph Harwood had made him a private offer of one thousand pounds for the recovery of the necklace of diamonds and rubies. Darling had landed in St. John's, on his quest, about six days before his meeting with Dick Lynch. Upon landing he had learned at the Merchants' Club that the *Royal William*, bound for New York from London, was reported lost. She had foundered in mid-ocean or had been shattered upon some desolate coast. The underwriters had paid up like men – and both the American and English press had lamented the tragic fate of Miss Flora Lockhart, the young New York singer, who had so lately won fame in London.

Darling had taken the news of Flora's terrible fate keenly to heart. He had crossed the ocean with her three years before; and she had haunted his dreams, waking and sleeping, ever since. Though he had always felt that his devotion was hopeless, it was no less real for that. And now, from a drunken fisherman, he had learned that she was alive, in good health, and a captive!

Mr. Darling went straight to his own hotel from the *Ship Ahoy*. He cleaned his pistols, made a rough map of the east coast, south of Witless Bay, from the information obtained from Dick Lynch, packed a couple of saddle-bags, rolled up a pair of blankets and sent for the landlord. From the landlord he obtained change for two five-pound Bank of England notes, information concerning the road from St. John's to the head of Witless Bay, and hired a horse.

Mr. Darling set out on his adventurous journey after an early breakfast eaten by candle-light. He felt courageous, invincible. He would rescue the lady of his long sea-dreams from that black-faced, black-hearted pirate who was called the skipper of Chance Along. In the flush of this determination the necklace was forgotten. So confident was he of success, and so intent upon picturing the rescue of that beautiful creature who had bewitched him three long, varied sailor-years ago, that he had covered several miles of his journey before noticing the stumblings and gruntings of the ill-conditioned beast between his knees. He departed from the city by way of a road leading westward from the head of the harbor. This he followed for three miles, through slush and half-frozen mud, then turned to the left. He forced his horse into a trot. It pecked badly, and he shot over its bowed head and landed in a mud-hole. Scrambling to his feet he noticed for the first time the gaunt ribs, heaving flanks and swollen legs of his steed. He swore heartily, seized the bridle and dragged the horse forward. The road was indescribable. Mud, slush, and icy water took him to the knee at every step; but he plugged manfully forward, dragging the protesting horse after him. So for an hour, across the barren rise of land to the southward, after which he remounted and rode at the best speed he could command until the horse stumbled again and again unseated him. Undaunted, Mr. Darling took his turn on foot again, dragging the puffing beast along at his muddy heels. The way was nothing but a muddy track across a desolate barren. It curved steadily to the left and at last brought him in sight of the irregular coast and the gray sea. By noon he had reached a miserable, dirty shebeen; and here he dried himself, sheltered and fed his horse and ate from his own provisions. He rested there for two hours (for his horse's sake rather than his own), and then mounted, threw a couple of shillings to the keeper of the house and continued on his way. He studied the coast-line intently as he floundered along. He saw that most of the shore ice had melted or broken away from the land-wash. Plans for the rescue of Flora Lockhart were taking shape in his mind. Beyond a doubt the rescue would have to be made by water; and so he studied every sheltered haven and surf-footed cape as he worked his heroic way southward, now plunging in his precarious saddle, now plunging with his own legs in the mire.

The figure of another wayfarer came in sight early in the afternoon. The stranger was on foot. He wore a red blanket round his shoulders and carried a long gun of ancient pattern. He was a big fellow with a swarthy face and bad eyes, and his ears were adorned with gold rings. Mr. Darling did not relish the fellow's looks, and so passed him without halting, alert, with his right hand on the butt of a pistol in his pocket. This picturesque ruffian was heading northward. After passing Mr. Darling he turned and glanced back several times, his interest doubtless attracted by the respectability of the other's appearance and the bulging saddlebags. But he did not stop. Neither did he return. The young man with the old horse looked to him like a fighter – and even if the saddle-bags were stuffed with gold they would prove but a flea bite to the stake which he had in mind.

Mr. Darling and his encumbering steed reached Raggedy Cove about an hour after sunset. Mr. Darling was in good heart and thanks to fine lungs and muscles, and a flawless constitution, was as fit in body as spirit. He found a bed for himself and a stable for the horse, and an old man full of information concerning the quickest and easiest way to get to Witless Bay. This was by water, said the old man. His own son George was going south along the coast next morning, in a bully. So Darling boarded the bully next morning, leaving his horse with the old man. George, the navigator of the bully, was an inquisitive young man; but his eyes were steady and his face honest. In spite of his prying questions, he won Mr. Darling's goodwill by the way he handled his boat. Of all branches of human skill, that of seamanship appealed most strongly to John Darling's heart and head. He respected a smart sailor just as intensely as he despised a bungling one. He was an unusually fine sailor himself, and could handle any vessel, large or small, as easily as he could navigate it. So he answered a few of the fisherman's questions good-naturedly, and asked a great many in return. George Wick had heard of Chance Along, but had never been there. And why should he have been there? Nobody ever went to Chance Along. Yes, he had once seen Black Dennis Nolan.

" 'Twas back in September, sir," he said. "Sure, didn't he put into Raggedy Cove one night – him an' his fore-an'-after – bound from St. John's, wid a freight o' grub an' gear. But what business would ye be havin' wid the likes o' him, sir?"

Darling ignored the question and asked another. No, George Wick was not familiar with the coast south of Witless Bay; but he had always heard that it was a desperate bad coast.

"What is your business in Witless Bay?" asked Darling.

The young fisherman pointed to four boxes of plug tobacco in the bottom of the bully.

"They bes for Skipper Walsh," he said. "I trades 'em for fish, an' then I heads back for Raggedy Cove."

"If you will sail me right around to Chance Along I will pay you well for it," said Darling. "My business in Chance Along is important – yes, very important. It would be worth five sovereigns to you, my man – that little trip."

George Wick looked interested, but shook his head.

"It bes a bad coast, sir," he said, "an' clean unbeknownst to me. An' now it would be desperate, sir, what wid the ice a-chokin' all the little coves so ye couldn't run in from a squall o' wind, sir."

"The shore-ice is gone, as you can see for yourself, and the drift-ice will not be down this way until near June," replied Darling. "But don't make any more excuses, George. You are not the man I want, anyway, for I see that you are no good for anything but asking questions. I'll be able to find some lad in Witless Bay, with a boat of some sort, who isn't afraid of the coast to the southward."

George Wick sulked for a few minutes, then asked, "What bes yer business wid Black Dennis Nolan, anyhow, sir? Bes ye a constable, sir, or anything like that?"

"My business is of a private nature," replied Mr. Darling. "I am a sailor, not a constable – an officer of the Merchant Marine."

"Aye, sir, I knowed ye for a sailor," said the other; "but there was a crew of constables along this way back in November, rigged out like fishermen an' swearin' as how they *was* fishermen. They went south; an' they soon come back wid empty hands. We was all t'inkin' in Raggedy Cove as how some vessel had maybe bin broke up afore it was deserted by the crew, as is the custom wid some folks in some harbors. An' when I see ye wid business in Chance Along, sir – well, Black Dennis Nolan do surely look to me like a man who'd be breakin' into a ship widout waitin' for her crew to desart her."

Mr. Darling smiled. "You are a smart man, George Wick," he said.

The bully rounded into Witless Bay and worked up to the settlement at the head of it without accident. Wick handed over his tobacco to Skipper Walsh; and then, with an eye on Mr. Darling, said he would call in a few days later for his trade of fish. Darling nodded, and purchased tea, hardbread and bacon from the skipper. Later, he and George filled a small keg with water and put it aboard, and bought two sealing-guns and a supply of powder and slugs. They headed down the bay at the first gray wash of dawn. After three hours of hauling across the wind they rounded the southern headland of the bay. They made an easting of more than a mile before heading due south. Mr. Darling took the tiller now, and George manned the sheet. Darling produced a pair of marine glasses and the chart which he had made from information received from Dick Lynch. They skirted a lee-shore and had to beat up to windward again and again to clear themselves. Before sunset they ran into a tiny, sheltered cove and made camp.

It was shortly after noon of the next day that Mr Darling, diligently scrutinizing the shore through his glasses, saw something that caught his attention. He edged the bully in and looked again.

"By heaven, it is a man's leg!" he exclaimed. He passed the glasses forward to Wick and pointed the direction.

"Sure," said Wick. "Sure, sir, it bes some poor divil wid a skinnywopper on his leg – so it bain't nobody from a wrack, ye kin lay to that."

They ran the bully shoreward and lowered the sail. Darling sprang to the land-wash and found the battered body of a man wedged tight between two icy rocks at the foot of the cliff. It was frozen stiff; but it was evident that it had not always been frozen. The crabs had found it, and even the heavy clothing was torn to strips. Mr. Darling stooped and took a little, red-bound casket from the torn breast. With his back to George Wick he opened it with trembling fingers. The diamonds and rubies of Lady Harwood's necklace flashed up at him!

M R. JOHN DARLING stood spellbound for a full half-minute, gazing down at the flaming, flashing gems coiled in their silken bed. He was aroused from his wonder and wild conjecture by the voice of George Wick.

"What bes the trouble, sir?" called the fisherman, who was busy fending the bully off the rocks. "Who bes it, anyhow? It bain't no friend o' yerself, sir, surely?"

Darling shut the casket and slipped it into an inner breast-pocket of his reefer. He turned slowly toward the sea and the boat, with a studied expression of puzzled pity on his face.

"Some poor fellow who has stepped off the cliff," he said. "I never saw him before – but the sight of him shook me a bit. He has been here quite awhile, I should say – yes, through thaw and frost, frost and thaw. Aye, and the crabs have been at him, poor devil! I suppose we should bury him; but there is no place here to dig a grave."

"Come aboard, sir! Come aboard wid ye!" exclaimed Wick, in a trembling voice. "It bain't no affair of our'n, sir – an' there bes the divil's own luck in finding a dead man unexpected."

Mr. Darling crossed the land-wash without another word, waded knee-deep into the tide, and climbed aboard the boat. George Wick poled the bully clear of the surf with one of the oars, then jumped forward and hoisted the red sail. Darling drew his chart from his pocket, examined it, then raised his glasses and studied the coast-line to the southward. The wind was light, but dead on shore. The bully hauled across it cleverly. A whitish gray haze stood along the sky-line to the east.

"We'll be havin' thick weather afore sundown, sir, wid this wind holdin'," said Wick.

Darling nodded. "We must be getting pretty close to Chance Along," he said. "Yes, there is smoke. Can you see it?"

George could not make it out with his unassisted eyes, but through the glasses he saw the blue reek of wood-smoke above a distant point of the coast easily enough. An hour later the bully threaded the rocks off Squid Beach. Dick Lynch had spoken of these rocks when the rum was warm in his head, in the tap-room of the *Ship Ahoy*, and Darling had marked them on his chart.

"We are within two miles of it," said Darling, his voice husky with emotion at thought of Flora Lockhart.

George Wick turned his face toward the east and the white wall of fog that now rolled upon the gray water within a mile of the coast.

"Aye, sir; but we'll not be makin' it afore the fog catches us," he replied.

"That will not bother my plans," said Darling. "I don't intend to sail right into Chance Along, anyway. I want to pay a surprise visit. We'll find a bit of a cove along here somewhere, I think."

He was right. About a mile and a half beyond the Squid Rocks they found a little sheltered cove that was no more than a pocket in the cliff. The beach was narrow, and a glance disclosed the fact that at every full tide it was entirely submerged; but a "drook" or a narrow cleft, thickly grown with hardy bushes, led up from the land-wash to the barrens above. They lowered the sail and nosed their way into the cove. The streaming skirmishers of the fog were over them by this time. They beached the bully at the foot of the drook and made her fast.

"Keep everything aboard, and make yourself snug," said Mr. Darling. "Watch the tide. Haul in and back off with it; and, whatever you do, lie low and keep quiet. I am going to take a look at Chance Along – on the sly, you understand. You'll know all about it later. Don't worry if I don't get back within the next two or three hours."

"Ye bes after Black Dennis Nolan, sir," said Wick.

Mr. Darling nodded, placed two loaded pistols in his pocket and vanished up the tangled slop of the drook. Wick listened to the upward scrambling until it suddenly died away and fog and silence covered him deep like a flood. Then he filled and lit his pipe and sat down in the shelter of a tarpaulin to think it over. He sensed danger in the blind choking air. He felt anxiety for his companion and fear for himself; but curiosity and a natural courage fortified him to a certain degree.

Upon reaching the level of the barrens, Mr Darling stood motionless for a little while and listened intently to the vague, fog-muffled breathing of the sea below him. He could hear nothing else. Turning to the south he moved silently forward along a well-worn path that traced the edge of the cliff. The fog was dense, and there was just enough wind to keep it drifting in from the sea. Darling held a boat-hook in his right hand and kept his eyes and ears alert. He heard a dog bark somewhere in front of him in the whitish-gray obscurity. Presently he came to where the path kinked and sloped down among a jumble of rocks, and at the same moment he caught the pungent, comforting smell of wood-smoke on the fog. Then he knew that Chance Along – the roof which sheltered Flora Lockhart – lay hidden and dripping beneath him. He was about to commence a cautious descent of the path, when a clamor of voices drifted up to him. He halted; and as the voices approached, together with the shuffle of climbing feet and the creak and clatter of shouldered boat-gear, he stepped aside. He saw the yellow blur of a lantern and immediately took up a position behind a great boulder. Bulky forms loomed into view at the top of the slope, broke from the blanketing fog for a moment, one by one, and plunged into it again, heading southward along the path. The big fellow in the lead carried the lantern, and the man at his elbow was talking excitedly as they passed within an oar's length of Darling.

"I's bin watchin' her these five hours back, skipper, a-tryin' to beat out o' the drift o' wind an' tide widout one entire mast a-standin'," he said. "She wasn't a half-mile off the rocks when I left the cove, an' a-firin' of her gun desperate. If she bain't stuck tight now, skipper, then me name bain't Tim Leary."

Mr. Darling stared and listened, as motionless as the boulder against which he leaned. They issued from the fog and were engulfed again in its clinging folds – twenty-five or thirty men and lads in all. Some carried coils of rope, others oars and boat-hooks. Several of them hauled empty sledges at their heels. The back of the last man vanished in the fog; but Mr. Darling remained in the shelter of the rock until the faintest whisper of their voices had died away before moving hand or foot.

"Organized wreckers," he muttered. "And that big pirate with the lantern was the skipper – the brute who is keeping Flora in this place! By God – I wonder just how much of a man, and how much of a beast he is! But now is my time, while they're all off waiting for another wreck to come ashore to them – damn them! The harbor must be about empty of able-bodied men just now."

He descended the twisting path cautiously. The small cabins

of the fishermen presently loomed around him, here a gray gable, there a dull window, there an unpainted door – and below him a roof or two pushing up through the fog from a lower terrace of the village. He groped his way about, pausing frequently to peer and hearken. From one cabin came the sound of a child crying angrily, from another the harsh coughing of some very old person, and from still another the whining of a dog. He moved to the left, feeling his way gingerly between the humble dwellings. A lighted window caught his attention, and then a man's voice, with a whimsical drawl and twang to it, raised in song.

Her eyes were like the sea in June,
Her lips was like a rose,
Her voice was like a fairy bell
A-ringin' crost the snows.
Then Denny, he forgot the wrack,
Forgot the waves a-rollin',
For she had put the witchy spell
On Skipper Dennis Nolan,

sang the voice behind the blurred yellow square of the window.

Darling approached the window on tip-toe and peered through the dripping glass. He saw that the vocalist was a long, thin fellow, with long, thin whiskers and a wooden leg, seated in a chair by a glowing stove. Two candles in tarnished brass sticks, a fiddle and bow, and a glass half full of red liquor that steamed, were on the corner of the deal table at his elbow. Beside him stood a young woman, long limbed, deep breasted, with a comely face that suggested cheeriness, but was now drawn and shadowed a little round the mouth and eyes with an expression of care. But it was a good face, trustworthy, kind and wise; and the man at the window trusted it the moment he saw it.

"I'll risk it," he muttered. "The old man looks harmless enough – and I might stumble around here until the fog lifts or the skipper gets back, without so much as a word with Flora, at this rate."

He withdrew from the window and slid quietly along the wall of the cabin until he found the door. He pulled the glove from his right hand and rapped on the wet planks with his bare knuckles. The voice of the man with the wooden leg

stopped dead in the middle of a line and shouted, "Come in."
Darling lifted the latch, pushed the door half open, and stepped
swiftly into the lighted room, closing the door smartly behind
him. The man and the girl stared at him in astonishment. He
removed his dripping cap from his head.

"Can you tell me where I can find Miss Flora Lockhart?" he
asked.

The man gasped at that, and the girl's gray eyes brightened.
The girl stepped forward, placed a strong, eager hand on his
arm and gazed into his face without apology or embarrassment.
Darling returned the scrutiny unabashed.

"Ye be from up-along?" she queried. "Ye be a friend o'
Flora's?"

"Yes," replied Darling. "I have heard that she is in this harbor
– and that no word of her being here, or even of her being
alive, has been sent out. Her friends believe her to be dead. And
I heard that the man you call skipper is – is keeping her against
her will. Of course, against her will! I have come to take her
away – back to the world in which she belongs."

"Be ye alone, sir?" asked Pat Kavanagh, combing his beard
with his long, lean fingers.

Darling frowned. "That's as may be," he said. "Alone or
not, I'm no such fool as to tell it until I know how I stand with
you; but I am armed, you may be sure!"

"Lad," said Pat, "I sees as how ye bes young, an' a sailor – aye,
an' bewitched, too. Sure, I was a sailor meself, in the old days.
I likes the cut o' yer fore-sils, lad, an' the lines o' yer hull, so I
tells ye, man to man like, watch out for the skipper. Aye, armed
or empty-handed, alone or wid a crew at yer back, watch out
for Black Dennis Nolan. He bes a grand lad in his own way, an'
ginerous an' fair wid his friends – but Saint Peter help the man
who hauls acrost his bows! If ye've come to Chance Along to
take the girl away wid ye, then get hold o' her quick an' clear
out wid her quick."

"I'll take ye to her, sir," said Mary, eagerly. "Come, sir!
Come along wid ye. She bes at the skipper's own house."

"At his own house? So I heard," said Darling, thickly.

"Aye," said Pat, "an' safe as if she was in church, wid Mother
Nolan to mind her. Sure, an' Denny Nolan bain't such a pirate
as ye t'inks, sir. Lie an' curse an' fight an' wrack he will, like
the divil himself; but he bes a decent man wid the helpless,
accordin' to his lights, for all that. Aye, cap'n, till she bes Denny

Nolan's wife she kin be any man's wife - if he bes smart enough to get her out o' Chance Along."

"Come along wid me, sir!" urged Mary, pulling at Darling's sleeve. "He bes out o' the harbor now, wid all the crew. Now bes yer chance, sir!"

She had thrown a shawl over her head and shoulders while her father was talking; and now she opened the door and led the sailor into the choking fog outside.

"Give me yer hand, sir, an' mind yer feet," she whispered. And then, as she pressed quickly forward, leading Darling by the hand, "It must be the saints themselves sent ye an' the fog to Chance Along together, sir – ye an' the fog an' the wrack they all bes a-lookin' out for!"

"Then I trust the saints may continue their good offices," said Darling, seriously.

"Aye, sir, an' why not?" she returned. "But here we be, sir. Mother Nolan an' yer lass bes alone in the house together this minute; an' Mother Nolan will not be sayin' nay to yer plans o' runnin' away."

She opened the door and drew Mr. Darling after her into the lighted kitchen. "Here bes yer help, Flora darlin'," she said. "An' 'twas no letter fetched him, ye kin lay to that, but the drag in his own heart for ye."

Old Mother Nolan looked up at them with her snapping black eyes.

"Shut the door!" said she. "D'ye want to fill all me poor old bones wid misery?"

Mary laughed uncertainly and slammed the door; and it was not until then that Flora Lockhart moved or uttered a sound. She sprang to her feet, her clear eyes shining like stars.

"Jack! Mr. Darling!" she cried. "You here? Have you come for me?"

The sailor's heart fairly flooded his arteries with joy and tenderness. She had remembered him at a glance after the three long years! She had called him by name! Work, ambition, fame and disaster had not driven out the memory of him.

"Yes, I have come for you," he said, huskily. "I would have come long ago if I had known – but I heard of it only by chance – a few days ago. Are you ready to come away with me now? We must hurry – for I fear that I am not strong enough to risk facing your jailer – just now."

Mother Nolan threw a fur coat about the girl's shoulders.

"Aye, she bes ready," said the old woman. "Mary, snatch her things together, an' carry 'em along. Step lively, for the love o' heaven! Have ye a boat, lad? Then get her to it as quick as ye kin, an' into it, an' away out o' Chance Along wid the two o' ye jist as quick as the holy saints will let ye!"

John Darling fastened the great coat around Flora with trembling fingers.

"To find you here!" he whispered. "And yet you seem nearer to me here than when I read of you – of your glory – out there in the great world."

Their hands touched. Her eyes kindled to his, flame to flame, throb for throb.

"I am glad – you have found me," she said. "You – you did not forget me."

At that moment the door was flung open and Black Dennis Nolan sprang into the room, followed closely by Bill Brennen and Nick Leary. The skipper had returned to the harbor because the ship in distress had drifted clear of the coast after all, and was even now firing her gun and burning her flares in clear water directly off Chance Along. Before flinging open the door the wreckers had seen through the window what was taking place in the kitchen.

Flora Lockhart screamed and flung her arms around John Darling, clinging to him as to her only hope of deliverance; and before he could pull himself clear of her and draw a pistol from his pocket the infuriated skipper was upon him. Nolan gripped with his left hand, and struck with his right fist and his whole body; but, quick as thought, the sailor twisted, ducked and gripped the other low about the hips. They hurtled across the room, collided against a chair and crashed to the floor with Darling on top. Bill Brennen plunged forward to help his master, but was met half-way by old Mother Nolan, who twined her claws in his whiskers and hung to him like a cat to a curtain. Nick Leary was about to settle things when Mary Kavanagh fell upon him with a leg of the broken chair. Flora alone did not join the fray. She fell back against the wall and covered her eyes with her hands.

Things were at a deadlock, with the chances good for Darling to break away from the dazed skipper and make his escape. Bill Brennen was of no use, for he could not strike the terrible old woman who hung to his whiskers until he yelled with the pain of it. Nick lay on the floor with music and stars in his head and conviction that Mary Kavanagh (who even now knelt on his chest) was a grand young woman entirely. Then young Cormick entered, took in the vital points of the situation at a glance, snatched up a stick of firewood, and jumped for the corner where his brother and the stranger lay clinched. Flora saw it from between her trembling fingers. She screamed and sprang forward with out-flung arms; but she was too late. The boy struck once with the billet – and the fight was ended.

FOR HALF a minute the skipper was mad enough to kill the unconscious sailor with his hands and feet; but Mother Nolan and Mary Kavanagh together were equal to the task of holding him and bringing him to a glimmering of reason. Mother Nolan's tongue did not spare him, even as her fingers had not spared poor, loyal Bill Brennen's whiskers.

"Would ye be murderin' him?" she cried. "An' him helpless – aye, an' a better man nor ye be yerself, Denny Nolan. Then ye be no blood an' kin to me, ye great murderer! Didn't he land ye on the flat o' yer great back, ye limb, though ye took him all suddant an' unawares? Sure, he did! Kill him, then; an' 'twill be your own father's mother goes to St. John's to bring the police to hang ye up by yer cowardly neck. Aye, ye kin lay to that! What old Kate Nolan says she says, an' the divil himself couldn't make a liar of her!"

"I thought ye was a man, Denny, an' fought like a man," said Mary Kavanagh, in a low voice that shook with unuttered sobs; "but if ye strikes him now, a-layin' there as harmless as a swile, then I'll know ye for a coward an' a murderer."

The skipper looked down at Flora Lockhart, who knelt above Darling, weeping bitterly. His black eyes glowed and his face twisted and paled.

"If it had bin meself hit the blow that downed him, then I'd be finishin' him," he said, "but I don't kill where I don't down! I bain't no coward, Mary Kavanagh, as well ye knows! Bes there any more o' the likes of him a-sneakin' 'round me own harbor?"

"He come alone," said Mary. "He come alone, to find the girl ye've bin hidin' an' holdin' in Chance Along till all her folks thinks she bes dead."

"Sure, then, he found her," snarled the skipper, "an' little good 'twill be doin' him!"

"Shame upon ye, Denny Nolan!" exclaimed the old woman. "Shame upon ye an' yer lies an' yer wicked, silly heart that t'ought to keep the likes o' her forever in Chance Along. Ye bain't able to fool old Kate Nolan wid yer lies! Sure, wasn't I on to ye from the minute ye come home that ye'd not bin to Witless Bay wid the letter? I seed the lie writ across yer face, Denny Nolan. Shame upon ye to be tryin' to bury the poor helpless girl alive!"

"Pick him up," said the skipper, sullenly. "There bes grub enough an' to spare to feed him an' a hundred like him. Heave him up atween ye, men, an' we'll be lockin' of him up in a safe place. Fetch along the lantern, Cormy, lad."

John Darling opened his eyes at this moment, stared dizzily around him and struggled up to one elbow.

"Flora!" he cried. "Flora, where are you?"

The girl tried to go to him, but the skipper held her. Bill Brennen pressed the sailor back, and tied his wrists and ankles.

"Who carried the letter out to him?" demanded the skipper, gripping the girl's shoulders with his great hands, and glaring down into her colorless face. For answer, she wrenched herself away, and struck him a stinging blow across the mouth with her right hand.

"How dare you?" she cried. "How dare you lay hands on me? I despise you, you brute!"

He stepped back, his face crimson, his mouth twitching, all the fire and mastery gone from his eyes. He had thought, poor fool, that she was learning to care for him; for of late, in her game of self-defence, she had treated him with evident consideration and many little attentions of the voice and eyes. And now he understood. He saw the truth in every flash of her eyes, in every line of brow, mouth and chin. He turned, took the lantern from Cormick and strode from the house, with Bill and Nick and their prisoner at his heels.

"Go down to the land-wash an' spy 'round for his boat," he said to Cormick. "Turn out a couple o' men to help ye hunt for it – an' maybe ye'll find some more o' these sneakin' robbers hangin' 'round the harbor."

They carried Darling to the store, the skipper leading the way, and his trusties swinging and hoisting their helpless burden by heels and shoulders. They dropped him on the cold floor as if he had no more feelings than a sack of hard bread.

"That bes all, lads," said the skipper. "Go help hunt for the boat now an' shut the door behind ye. I'll jist be sayin' a few words to this dirty spy afore I leaves him to his dreams."

Brennen and Leary turned and left the store without a word.

They felt vaguely uneasy, as if the great world of up-along had at last found them out, and reached a menacing hand into their snug harbor. Would the skipper be able to deal with so vast an enemy? If he killed this stranger it would mean hanging by the neck, sooner or later – perhaps for every man in the harbor? If he let him live, and held him a prisoner, it would bring the law prying into their affairs, some time or other. Doubt chilled them. They stumbled heavily away in the darkness.

The skipper held the lantern to his captive's face and regarded him with wolfish, sneering attention. Soon the sneer faded a little.

"I's seed ye afore," he said. "Aye, sure as hell, I's seed ye afore!"

"And this is not the first time I've seen *your* ugly mug, either," returned Darling. "I saw you that night the *Durham Castle* came ashore on this coast – the night you robbed the captain and the passengers. Well, what are you going to do about it?"

"Ye'll larn that soon enough," returned the other. "Did ye get a letter from – from her?"

"No," replied Darling, unable to see any danger in telling the truth of that matter. "No, I didn't get any letter. I met a friend of yours in St. John's, and he told me a great deal about you, and the game you are playing in this harbor – and also about her. Your friend's name is Dick Lynch."

"Dick Lynch," repeated the skipper, quietly. "I'll be cuttin' the heart out o' that dog yet!"

"And a good job, no doubt," said Darling. "But I warn you, my man, that if you injure Miss Lockhart in any way you'll curse the day you first saw daylight. You'll be burned out of here like the dirty, murdering pirate that you are – you and your whole crew. The law will have you, my man – it will have you by the neck. Do you think I risked coming to this place without leaving word behind me of where I was bound for and what I was after?"

"Now ye be lyin'," said the skipper, coolly. "Ye telled the truth about Dick Lynch; but now ye lie. Don't ye try to fool wid me, damn ye! Ye come to Chance Along widout leavin' a word behind ye. I sees the lie in yer face."

"I left Dick Lynch behind me," said the sailor.

That shook the skipper's assurance; but he was in no mood to feel fear for more than a moment. He laughed sneeringly and began to unload his captive's pockets. He took out the pistols, admired them and laid them aside. Next, he unearthed a few cakes of hard bread, a small flask of brandy, and a pipe and half a plug of tobacco.

"How'd ye come to Chance Along, anyhow? Where bes yer boat?" he asked, suddenly, pausing in his work.

"I walked across from Witless Bay," said Darling.

"Where bes yer boat?" asked the other.

"In Witless Bay, you fool! Do you think I carried it across my back?"

The skipper swung the lantern back and glanced at the soles of the other's boots.

"Ye bes a liar – and a desperate poor one at that," he said. "Where bes yer boat?"

John Darling lost his temper. He disliked being forced into telling a lie – and, being human, he disliked still more to have the lie discovered and the effort wasted.

"Go to hell and find it, you black-faced pirate!" he roared.

The skipper stopped, glared down at him, and swung his right hand back for a blow.

"Hit away, I'm tied," said the other, without flinching.

The skipper let his hand sink to his side.

"I don't hit a tied man. That bain't my way," he said, flushing darkly.

"Untie me, then, and you can hit all you want to. Cut these ropes and let me at you. Come now, for I see that you have some sense of manliness in you, after all."

"Not jist now. To-morrow, maybe – or maybe next day – I'll fight ye. And, by hell, when I do I'll kill ye wid me two hands!"

"I'll take the chance. Unless you starve me or cripple me in the meantime, I'll knock the everlasting life out of you."

The skipper growled and took up his interrupted work of investigating the other's pockets. He unbuttoned the heavy reefer and thrust a hand into an inner pocket. In a second he withdrew it, holding the little casket bound in red leather. A cry of astonishment escaped him. He pressed the catch with his thumb and the diamonds and rubies flashed and glowed beneath his dazzled eyes.

"Me own diamonds!" he cried. "Holy saints alive, me own diamonds! Where'd ye find 'em? Tell me that, now – where'd ye find 'em?"

Darling did not reply for a moment. Then, speaking quietly

and somewhat bitterly, he said, "If you really want to know, I found them on a dead man, under the cliff a few miles to the north of here."

"That would be Foxey Jack Quinn," said the skipper. He closed the box and put it in his pocket, then took up the lantern and went out, locking the door behind him.

In the meantime, Mary Kavanagh had not been idle. She felt sure that the stranger was safe from bodily harm for the night at least, now that Dennis had shaken off the first blind deviltry of his rage. She knew Dennis almost as well as old Mother Nolan did; and to-night she felt sorry for him as well as angry with him. Leaving Flora in Mother Nolan's care, she left the house, and followed Cormick and the others down to the land-wash. The fog was thinning swiftly; but night had fallen, and the sky, sea and land were all black as tar. She soon learned that no sign of the stranger's boat could be found in the harbor. Returning from the land-wash, she met Nick Leary.

"How bes ye a-feelin' now?" she asked, not unkindly. "But it served ye right, Nick. A great man like ye has no call to be fightin' wid women."

"Me poor head buzzes like a nest o' wasps whin ye pokes it wid a club," said Nick. "Sure, Mary, 'twas a sweet tap ye give me! Marry me, girl, an' ye'll be free to bat me every day o' yer born life."

"Sure, an' 'twould do ye no harm," said Mary. And then, "So ye've shut the poor lad in the store, have ye?"

"Aye, but how'd ye know it, Mary?"

"I didn't know it, Nick, till ye telled me. Now go on wid yer business o' huntin' for the boat an' I'll be goin' on wid mine. An' thanks for yer offer, lad; but sure I'll never marry a man I kin knock down wid the leg o' a chair."

Nick seemed to be in no mood to accept this statement as final; but the girl soon cleared her tracks of him in the inky darkness, among the little houses. She climbed the path to the edge of the barren and turned northward. From what she had seen of John Darling she felt sure that he was no fool; and therefore she had not expected to find his boat in the harbor. He had told Mother Nolan that he had a boat, but had not mentioned its whereabouts. Mary decided that it was hidden somewhere handy to the harbor; and she was inclined to think that it was manned. He had come from the north, of course; therefore the chances were good that he had left his boat somewhere to the north of the harbor. She knew every hollow, break and out-thrust of that coast for miles as well as she knew the walls and floors of her father's cabin. A thought of the little drook came to her mind and she quickened her steps along the path. The light wind was shifting and the fog was trailing coastwise to the south before it. Mary noted this, sniffed at the air, which was slowly but surely changing in quality, and looked up at the black sky.

"There'll be snow afore mornin'," she said.

When she reached the head of the drook she halted and gave ear. The sloshing and lapping of the tide came up to her; and that was all for a minute or two. She parted the alders and young birches with her hands, very cautiously, and moved downward into the thicket for a distance of three or four yards, then halted again and again listened. At last, above the noises of the tide and almost smothered by them, she heard a sound unmistakably human – a violent sneeze. For a little while she remained quiet, daunted by the darkness and trying to consider the risks she was about to take. But the risks could not be considered, for they were absolutely unknown. She was playing for peace and justice, however – yes, and for Denny Nolan's happiness. Mastering her fear, she whistled softly. After a minute's silence a guarded voice replied to the whistle.

"Be that yerself, sir?" inquired the voice from the blackness below.

She descended lower, parting the tangled growth before her with her hands.

"I bes a friend – an' a woman," she said. "I comes wid a word for ye, from him."

"Stand where ye bes!" commanded George Wicks, his voice anxious and suspicious. "What the divil bes the trouble now? Stand where ye bes an' tell me the word."

"I bes all alone, so help me Peter!" replied the girl, "an' it bain't safe the way we bes talkin' now, up an' down the drook. The lads o' the harbor may be comin' this way an' a-hearin' us – an' then ye'll bes in as bad a way as the captain himself. Let me come down to ye. Bes ye afeared o' one lone woman?"

"Come down wid ye, then," said George, his voice none too steady, "but I warns ye as how I hes a lantern here an' a pistol, an' if ye bain't all alone by yerself I'll shoot ye like a swile an' ax ye yer business afterwards. I's heard queer t'ings o' Chance Along!"

"I bes alone," returned Mary, "an' if ye fires yer pistol at me then ye bes a dirty coward."

As she spoke she continued her difficult way down the channel of the drook. She saw the yellow gleam of the lantern between the snarled stems of the bushes. Strong, clear-headed and brave as she was, she began now to sob quietly with fright; yet she continued to push her way down the drook.

"They – they has caught the captain," she said brokenly, "an' now they bes huntin' all 'round the harbor for his boat. I has – come to tell ye – an' to help ye."

George Wicks parted the bushes, raised his lantern and peered up at her.

"There bain't no call for ye to be cryin'," he said, in a changed voice. "If ye means no treachery, lass, then I'll not be hurtin' ye."

She stood beside him; and as he stared at her by the yellow light of the lantern all thought of treachery from that quarter faded away. His heart warmed and got a trifle out of hand. He could scarcely believe his senses, and for a moment forgot John Darling and the queer stories he had heard of Chance Along. All he realized was that his eyes and the lantern told him that the finest looking girl he had ever seen had come down the drook, all of her own free will, to pay him a visit.

"The skipper caught him an' tied him up in the store," whispered Mary, "an' now all the men in the harbor bes searchin' for the boat." Then she told the story of Flora Lockhart, and disclosed a plan for outwitting the skipper that had just come to her mind.

"Sure, ye bes a wonder," said George, who was as clay in her hands. "Aye, we'll be putting the comather on to Black Denny Nolan, ye kin lay to that! Sure, it be a grand idee altogether!"

So they unloaded the bully and hid everything among the bushes.

"Now you must lay low," cautioned Mary, "an' I'll bring yer bully back to ye as soon as I kin – or maybe one o' the skipper's bullies in its place. Anyhow, I'll get to see ye agin to-morrow night. Lay low, now, an' don't be lightin' a fire."

As she stepped aboard the bully George's mind cleared a little.

"Ye bain't playin' any tricks on me, I do hope," he whispered. "Ye wouldn't be leavin' me here all alone by meself forever, widout me bully even, would ye now?"

"Ye kin trust me," said Mary. Then she shoved off into the darkness.

Half an hour later the keel of the bully touched the land-wash in the sheltered harbor of Chance Along. Mary Kavanagh stepped ashore, laid the oar noiselessly inboard and set the bully adrift, and then made her cautious way up and into her father's cabin. Snow began to fall thickly and silently as she closed the door.

JOHN DARLING was sore, hungry and cold; but his heart was joyful and strong. He had been knocked over the head, and he had been robbed of the newly-recovered necklace and the reward of a thousand pounds; but he had found Flora, alive, evidently not ill-treated and not in any real danger save of oblivion, and with the memory of him clear in her heart. He had failed to get her away from the harbor; but he felt convinced that a way of escape for both of them would soon occur. He did not fear Black Dennis Nolan. The fellow was a man, after all. He knew that if he should come to any serious physical injury at the skipper's hands it would be in a fair fight. Also, he knew that Mother Nolan and Mary Kavanagh were on his side – were as anxious to get Flora out of the harbor as he was to take her out. But the planks upon which he lay were as cold and hard as ice; and at last he began to wonder if even his splendid constitution would stand a night of this exposure, bound hand and foot, without serious results. He lay awake for hours, suffering in body but rejoicing in heart. At last, numb with cold, he sank into a half-doze. He was aroused by sounds at the door – the cry of a key turning an unoiled lock and the creak of rusty hinges. Then the welcome gleam of a lantern flooded to him along the frosty floor. The visitor was Bill Brennen. He stooped above the sailor and squinted at him curiously. Under his left arm he carried a caribou skin and several blankets.

"Lad," said he, "ye must be full o' the divil's own ginger to cross the skipper as ye done. Sure an' the wonder bes why he didn't kill ye dead! But now that ye still be alive, him not killin' ye in the first flush, ye bes safe as Mother Nolan herself. A divil o' a woman that, entirely. Saints in glory, me whiskers still aches desperate! Here bes a grand rug for ye to lay on, an' blankets to cover yerself wid. The skipper sent 'em. Kill a man he will, in fair fight; but it bain't in his nature to let any man go cold nor hungry in Chance Along."

He spread the caribou skin and one of the blankets on the floor and rolled John Darling on to them. Then he threw two more blankets over him and tucked them in. Next, he produced a flask from his pocket and uncorked it.

"Skipper's orders," he said, and held the flask to the helpless one's lips.

"Now ye bes as snug as any marchant, what wid yer grand bed an' yer drop o' fine liquor in yer belly," he remarked. He turned at the door and said, "Some one will be bringin' ye grub in the mornin'. Good night to ye."

From that until morning, the prisoner on the floor, bound at wrist and ankle, rested more peacefully than Black Dennis Nolan in his father's bed; for the sailor was only sore in his muscles and bones, but the skipper ached in heart and soul. The skipper tossed through the black hours, reasoning against reason, hoping against hopelessness. The girl hated him and despised him! Twist and turn as he might, he could not escape from this conviction. Now he even doubted the power of the diamonds and rubies to win her, having seen that in her eyes which had brought all his dreams crumbling to choking dust. Pain had laid the devil of fury in him and aroused the imp of stubbornness. He would wait and watch. He was safe to keep them both in the harbor until the arrival of Father McQueen, in June; and perhaps, by that time, he would see some way of winning the girl. Should the necklace of diamonds and rubies fail to impress the girl, then he might bribe John Darling with it to leave the harbor. You see, the workings of the skipper's mind were as primitive as his methods of coping with mutineers.

The skipper left his bed and the house at the first gray of dawn, determined to search the coast high and low for a solution of the mystery of the stranger's arrival. He went down between the silent cabins, all roofed with new snow, and the empty snow-trimmed stages, and looked out upon the little harbor. What was that, just at the edge of the shadow of the rock to the right of the narrow passage? – a boat, lump of wreckage or a shadow? Stare as he would, he could not determine the nature of the thing in that faint and elfin twilight; but it drew his eye and aroused his curiosity as no natural shadow of any familiar rock could have done. He dragged a skiff from under one of the stages and launched it into the quiet harbor and with a single oar over the stern sculled out toward the black object on the steel-gray tide. It proved to be a fine bully, empty and with the frozen painter hanging over the bow and trailing alongside.

"So this bes how he come to Chance Along — an' not man enough to moor his boat safe!" exclaimed the skipper.

The bully was as empty as on the day it had been built, save for one oar lying across the thwarts. Not even a spar and sail were aboard her. The man must be an absolute fool to set out along a dangerous coast, in a bad time of year, single-handed and without grub or gear, reflected the skipper. The thought that such a bungler as this stranger should be preferred to himself, intensified his pangs of humiliation. No girl who understood such things — no girl of that coast — would treat him so, he reflected, bitterly. He pulled the dripping painter aboard the skiff, made it fast around a thwart and towed the bully ashore.

Mary Kavanagh had been astir as early as the skipper himself. She had gone first to the store. Peering through a window, she had made out the stranger's form on the floor, bulkily blanketed. From the store, she hastened to the skipper's house, saw his footprints pointing toward the land-wash, and stood with her hand on the latch until a skiff slid out into her line of vision from behind the drying-stages. She knew that the skipper was on his way to investigate the derelict bully. She opened the door then, entered quietly and went to Mother Nolan's room. The old woman was sitting up in bed with her nightcap a-tilt over one ear.

"Saints alive, Mary, what mischief bes afoot now?" asked Mother Nolan.

Mary drew close to the bed-side and leaned over to her confederate.

"The captain bes safe in the store, all rolled up in blankets," she whispered, "an' — an' I larned something last night that means as how we kin get 'em both away before long, wid luck. An' I played a trick on the skipper — so don't ye bes worryin' when he tells ye as how he's found the captain's boat. Give the word to the lass to keep her heart up. Sure, we'll be gettin' the two o' them safe out o' the harbor yet."

"An' where bes Denny now? How'd ye get into the house?" asked the old woman.

"He bes out in a skiff this very minute, a-lookin' at the captain's boat where it bes driftin' 'round the harbor. Sure, an' that bes just where I wants him. An' now I'll be goin', Mother Nolan dear, for I bain't wishin' Denny to catch me here awhisperin' t'ye so early in the mornin' or maybe he'd get the idea into his head as how us two women bain't such harmless fools as what he's always bin takin' us for."

"Ye bes a fine girl, Mary Kavanagh," returned Mother Nolan, "an' I trusts ye to clear this harbor o' trouble. I'll be tellin' the good word to the poor lass inside this very minute. Her heart bain't all diamonds an' pride, after all, as she let us know last night, poor dear."

Mary left them, and a minute later met the skipper on his way up from the land-wash.

"I's found the boat the stranger come in," said the skipper.

"Sure, an' so ye would, Denny, if it was to be found," replied Mary.

The young man eyed her gloomily and inquiringly until she blushed and turned her face away from him.

"Ye talks fair, Mary," he said. "Ye talks as if ye was a friend o' mine; but ye bain't always actin' that same way, these days. Last night, now, ye an' granny was sure fightin' agin me! I seed ye bat Nick Leary wid the leg o' the chair – an' I seed that dacent old woman a-hangin to Bill Brennen's whiskers like a wildcat to the moss on a tree."

"An' why not, Denny Nolan?" retorted the girl. "Ye t'ree men was after murderin' that poor lad! D'ye think Mother Nolan was wantin' to see ye carried off to St. John's an' hung by yer neck? Sure, we was fightin' agin ye. What hurt had that poor lad ever done to ye? He come to Chance Along looking for his lass – an' sure, she was ready enough to be goin' away wid him!"

The skipper's face darkened. "Who saved her life from the wrack?" he cried. "Tell me that, will ye! Who salvaged her from the foretop o' the wrack?"

Without waiting for an answer, he brushed past Mary and strode up to his house. The girl stood motionless for a little while, gazing after him with a flushed face, twitching lips and a flicker of amusement in her gray eyes.

"Poor Denny," she murmured. "His pride bes hurt more nor the heart of him!"

John Darling was not honored by a visit from the skipper that day; but Bill Brennen carried food to him, made up a fire in the stove, and even loosed his bonds for a few minutes upon receiving his word of honor that he would not take advantage of the kindness by trying to escape.

"What does Nolan intend to do with me?" asked Darling.

"Well, sir, it looks to me as how he bes figgerin' to keep ye in Chance Along till June. He bes t'inkin' as how the young lady may blow 'round to his own idee," replied Bill.

"And what is his idea?"

"As how he bes a better man nor ye be."

"But why does he figure to keep me until June? Why not until July, or August – or next Christmas?"

"Well, sir, ye see it bes this way wid him. Father McQueen, the dear, riverent gentleman – an' may he never die till I kills him, an' may every blessed hair on his head turn into a wax candle to light him to glory! – bes comin' back to Chance Along in June. The skipper bain't afeared o' any man in the world but his riverence."

John Darling smiled. "I should like to see Father McQueen," he said; "but I am afraid I must be going away from here considerably before the first of June."

Bill wagged his head. "Now don't ye be too sure, sir," he whispered. "Ye bain't dealin' wid any ignorant fisherman when ye bes dealin' wid Black Dennis Nolan. Sure, didn't he find yer bully this very mornin'!"

"My bully!" exclaimed the other, losing color. "Where did he find it?"

"Driftin' in the harbor," returned Bill. "It bes a grand bully entirely, sir."

Darling was silent for a moment. Then, trying to look as if the finding of the bully drifting in the harbor was rather a joke, he laughed.

"And did he capture my crew of five strong men?" he asked.

Bill Brennen grinned. "Now ye needn't be tryin' any o' yer divilment on me," he said. "The bully was as empty as Tim Sullivan's brain-locker – an' the holy saints knows as that bes empty enough! Sure, there wasn't even a sail aboard her, nor a bite o' grub nor a drop o' liquor."

"My five men must have fallen overboard," said Darling, smiling. Poor John! Now, should he manage to escape and get Flora out of the skipper's house, how was he to get out of the harbor? What had happened to George Wick? The tide must have carried the bully out of the drook, while George was asleep, and drifted it around to the harbor. He promised himself the pleasure of teaching Master George the art of mooring a boat if he ever met him again.

John Darling spent an anxious day. Shortly after midnight he was startled by a faint tapping on one of the windows. The night was pitch black, and so he could see nothing. The tapping was repeated. He rolled out of his blanket and across the floor toward the sound. His progress was arrested by a rank of boxes and flour-bags. Pressing his shoulder against these, he hitched himself to his feet, turned and leaned across them until his face was within a foot of the faint square of the window. Against the half-darkness he could now see something indistinct in shape, and all of a dense blackness save for a pale patch that he knew to be a human face. It was Mary Kavanagh. She told him briefly of the way she had turned the skipper from searching the coast for his boat and his companion; of Flora's safety, and of how she hoped to accomplish their escape before long – perhaps on the following night. Wick was still hidden in the drook, she said. She would try to get a boat of some kind around to him on the next night; and if she succeeded in that, she would return and try to get Darling out of the store and Flora out of the skipper's house.

The sailor was at a loss for words in which to express his gratitude.

"But ye must promise me one thing," whispered the girl. "Ye must swear, by all the holy saints, to do naught agin Denny Nolan when once ye git safe away – swear that neither Flora nor yerself puts the law on to Denny, nor on to any o' the folks o' this harbor, for whatever has been done."

"I swear it, by all the saints," replied Darling. "For myself – but I cannot promise it for Flora. You must arrange that with her."

Several hours after Mary's interview with John Darling, old Mother Nolan awoke in her bed, suddenly, with all her nerves on the jump. The room was dark, but she felt convinced that a light had been held close to her face but a moment before. She felt no fear for herself, but a chilling anxiety as to what deviltry Denny might be up to now. Could it be that she was mistaken in him after all? Could it be that he was less of a man than she had thought? She crawled noiselessly from her bed and stole over to the door of Flora Lockhart's room. The door was fastened. With the key, which she had brought from under her pillow, she made sure that it was locked. She unlocked it noiselessly, opened the door a crack and peered in. The room was lighted by the glow from the fire and by a guttering candle on a chair beside the bed. She saw that the room was empty, save for the sleeping girl. Closing the door softly and locking it again, she turned and groped her way across to the kitchen door, beneath which a narrow line of light was visible. Scarcely breathing, she raised the latch, drew the door inward a distance of half an inch and set one of her bright old eyes to the crack. She saw the skipper kneeling in a corner of the kitchen, with his back to her and a candle on the floor beside him. He seemed to be working busily and heavily, but not a sound of his toil reached her eager ears.

"He bes hidin' somethin'," she reflected. "Shiftin' some o' his wracked gold, maybe? But why bes he so sly about it to-night, a-spyin' in on his old grandmother to see if she bes sound asleep or no?"

Presently, she closed the door and crept back to her bed. Next morning, as soon as the skipper and young Cormick had left the house, she examined the corner of the floor where the skipper had been at work. She had to pull aside a wood-box to get at the spot. One of the narrow, dusty planks showed that it had been tampered with. She pried it up with a chisel, dug into the loose earth beneath and at last found a small box covered with red leather. She opened it and gazed at the diamonds and rubies in frightened fascination. Ignorant as she was of such things, she knew that the value of these stones must be immense. At last she closed the casket, returned it to the bottom of the hole and replaced the earth, the plank and the wood-box. Where, when and how had the skipper come by that treasure? she wondered. She hobbled over to Pat Kavanagh's house and told Mary all about it.

Pierre Benoist, the survivor of the French brig, arrived at Mother McKay's shebeen in good order, with the borrowed blanket draped over his broad shoulders and the borrowed sealing-gun under his arm. All birds of Pierre's variety of feather seemed to arrive naturally at Mother McKay's, sooner or later. The French sailor found Dick Lynch; a Canadian trapper with Micmac blood in his veins, who had come out of the woods too soon for his own good; three men from Conception Bay and half a dozen natives of the city, all talking and swearing and drinking Mother McKay's questionable rum and still more questionable whiskey. Pierre laid aside his blanket and musket, shouted for liquor and then studied the assembled company. It did not take him long to decide that they were exactly the material he required. He took a seat at Dick Lynch's elbow and in such English as he was master of, remarked that any man who worked for his living was no better than a fool.

"Sure," said Lynch, "by the looks o' yerself ye should know."

Monsieur Benoist pulled his sinister mouth into as pleasant a grin as he could manage, and veiled the dangerous light in his eyes. Then he replied, in a loud voice that caught the attention of all the men in the room, that he was certainly in a position to know, having come straight from a little harbor to the southward where a handful of fishermen had just salvaged two chests of good French gold from a wreck. He told the whole story of the wreck and of the subsequent fight in which his companion had been killed. To add reality to his tale he described several of the fishermen minutely.

"That bes the skipper himself!" cried Dick Lynch. "That bes Black Dennis Nolan, ye kin lay to that – aye, an' Bill Brennen an' Nick Leary! Sure, then, ye've come from Chance Along, b'y – the very place I comes from meself. Two chests o' gold, d'ye say? Then I tells ye, b'ys, there bes as much more there besides. Chance Along bes fair stinkin' wid gold an' wracked stuff."

He went on excitedly and gave a brief and startling outline

of the recent history of Black Dennis Nolan and Chance Along, not forgetting his own heroic stand against the tyrant.

"B'ys, all we has to be doin' bes to go an' take it – an' then to scatter. This here captain wid the rings in his ears has the right idee, sure! Wid all the gold an' jewels in Chance Along shared amongst us sure we'd never be needin' to hit another clip o' work so long as we live. Aye, 'twould be easy wid guns in our hands; but we must be quick about it, lads, or the law'll be gittin' there ahead o' us," he concluded.

The others clustered about Lynch and the French sailor, a few of them reeling, but all intent upon coming to some arrangement for laying hands upon the treasure of Chance Along. Big fists pounded the sloppy table, husky voices bellowed questions, and stools and benches were overturned.

"There bes twelve o' us here,' said Tom Brent, of Harbor Grace, "twelve able lads, every mother's son o' us ready for to make the trip. Now the first thing bes for every man to tell his name an' swear as how he'll do his best at gettin' the stuff an' never say naught about it to any livin' soul after he's got safe away wid his share."

All agreed to these suggestions, and oaths were taken and hopes of everlasting salvation pledged that were not worth the breath that sounded them. It was next ascertained by Monsieur Benoist, who naturally took a leading part in the organization, that every man of the twelve possessed a fire-arm of one kind or another. Then Bill McKay, Mother McKay's son, and two others departed in quest of horses and sleds. The roads were fairly good now, though unpacked. Mother McKay set to work at the packing of provisions for the expedition. She was heart and soul in the enterprise, and would have her interests represented by her son Bill, the worst rascal, hardest fighter and most devoted son in St. John's. She had a hold on some of the small farmers around – in fact, she owned several of the farms – so it was not long before Bill and his companions returned, each in possession of a horse and sled. The expedition set out at two o'clock of a windless, frosty, star-lit morning. They travelled the roads which John Darling had followed, several days before; but now the mud-holes and quaking bogs were frozen and covered with snow. Bill McKay drove the sled that led the way at a pace that gave the following teamsters all they could do to keep in touch; but willing hands manned the whips and hammering sled-stakes. Now and again one or another of the raiders would fall off a sled and necessitate a halt; and so the poor horses were given a chance, now and again, to recover something of their lost wind.

Back in Chance Along things were going briskly. Mary Kavanagh learned from John Darling something of the history of the diamond and ruby necklace and made up her mind to return it to the sailor. She wanted to clean the harbor of everything of the kind – of everything that came up from the sea in shattered ships, except food. She saw the hands of the saints in salvaged provisions, but the hand of the devil himself in wrecked gold and jewels – and wrecked women. She decided to arrange the recovery of the necklace and the bully, and the escape of the strangers for that very night; and her decision was sealed, a few hours later, by the skipper's behavior. It was this way with the skipper. He felt shame for having kept the girl in the harbor against her prayers, and for the lies he had told her and the destruction of the letters; but he was neither humble nor contrite. Shame was a bitter and maddening emotion for one of his nature. He brooded over this shame, and over that aroused by the girl's scorn, until his finer feelings toward her were burned out and blown abroad like ashes. His infatuation lost its fine, ennobling element of worship, and fell to a red glow of desire of possession. He forced his way to Flora's room, despite the protests of Mother Nolan.

"To-morrow ye'll be mine or ye'll be his," he said, staring fixedly at the frightened girl. "To-morrow mornin' him an' me bes a-goin' to fight for ye – an' the man what lives will have ye! Ye put the name o' coward on to me – but I bain't no coward! I fights fair – an' the best man wins. I could kill him now, if I was a coward."

Flora's face was as white as the pallid figure on the cross above the chimney.

"You *are* a coward! – and a beast!" she cried from dry lips. "If you kill him my curse shall be with you until your dying day – and afterwards – forever."

"Then ye can tell him to go away, an' I won't be killin' him," said the man.

"Tell him – to go – away?"

"Aye – that ye've no need o' him. Send him away. Tell him ye means to marry wid me."

"No," whispered the girl. And then, "Do you mean to – give him a chance? – to fight him fair?"

"Aye, man to man – an' as sure as the divil fetched him to Chance Along I'll kill him wid these hands! An' then – an' then ye'll be mine – an' when Father McQueen comes in June 'twill be time for the weddin' – for that part o' it. Ye've put the names o' coward an' beast on to me – an' by Saint Peter, ye'll live to change them names or to know them!"

Some color came back to Flora's cheeks and her clear eyes shone to their depths.

"If you fight fair," she said, faintly but steadily, "he will give you what you deserve. I am not afraid. God will be with him – and he is the better man!"

The skipper laughed, then stooped suddenly, caught her in his arms and kissed her on the lips. Next moment he flung her aside and dashed from the room, almost overturning Mother Nolan in his flight. At the door of the kitchen he came face to face with Mary Kavanagh. He tried to pass her without pausing, but she stood firm on the threshold and held him for a moment or two with her strong arms. Her gray eyes were blazing.

"I sees the Black One a-ridin' on yer back!" she cried, in a voice of horror and disgust. "I sees his face over yer shoulder – aye, an' his arm around yer neck like a rope!"

He looked at her for a moment, and then quickly away as he forced her violently aside.

"An' the hell-fire in yer eyes!" she cried.

The skipper was free of her by then and out of the house; but he turned and stared at her with a haggard face and swiftly dulling eyes.

"The curse bes on me!" he whispered. "It bes in me vitals now – like I had kilt him already."

The expression of the girl's face changed in a flash and she sprang out and caught one of his hands in both of hers.

"Kill him? Ye bain't meanin' to kill him, Denny Nolan?" she whispered.

"Aye, but I bes, curse or no curse," he said, dully. "To-morrow mornin' I bes a-goin' to kill him – man to man, in fair fight."

"But for why, Denny?"

"For the girl."

"Bes ye lovin' her so desperate, Denny?"

"Nay, nay, lass, not now. But I wants her! An' she puts the name o' beast on to me an' the nature o' beast into me, like a curse!"

"To-morrow? An' ye'll fight him fair, Denny?"

"Aye, to-morrow – man to man – wid empty hands!"

The girl turned and entered the house, and the skipper went up the path at the back of the harbor and wandered over the snowy barrens for hours. It was dusk when Bill Brennen found him.

"Skipper," said Bill, "the lads bes at it again. They wants to know when ye'll make a trip to St. John's wid the jewels? – an' where the jewels bes gone to, anyhow?"

"Jewels!" cried the skipper – "an' the entire crew o' 'em fair rotten wid gold! I'll dig up the jewels from where we hid 'em an' t'row 'em into their dirty faces – an' they kin carry 'em to St. John's an' sell 'em to suit themselves, the squid!"

So he and Bill Brennen tramped off to the northward; and Mary Kavanagh was aware of their going.

Mary was busy during their absence. She unearthed the necklace, and with it and the key from behind the skipper's clock, made her way to the store. It was dark by now, with stars in the sky and a breath of wind from the south and south-by-west. The folks were all in their cabins, save the skipper and Bill Brennen, who were digging the harbor's *cache* of jewelry from the head of a thicket of spruce-tuck. She let herself into the store and freed John Darling without striking a light. She placed the casket in his hand.

"The skipper has yer pistols in his own pocket, so I couldn't git 'em for ye," she whispered. "Now sneak up to the back, quick. Ye'll find yer lass there, a-waitin' for ye wid old Mother Nolan. Git north to the drook where yer man bes, an' lay down there, the three o' ye, till I fetches yer bully. Then git out, an' keep out, for the love o' mercy! Step lively, captain! The skipper bes out o' the harbor this minute, but he bes a-comin' home soon. Get along wid ye quick, to the top o' the cliff."

She left him before he had an opportunity to even try to thank her. He followed her to the door, walking stiffly, paused outside for long enough to get his bearings, then closed the door noiselessly, turned the key in the lock, withdrew it and dropped it in the snow. Then he made his way cautiously to the back of the harbor and up the twisting path as fast as he could scramble. At the top, crouched behind a boulder, beside old Mother Nolan, he found Flora.

Neither the girl nor the man heard the old woman's words of farewell. They moved northward along the snowy path, hand in hand, running with no more sound than slipping star-shadows. So for a hundred yards; and then the speed began to slacken, and at last they walked. They reached the black crest where the brushwood of the drook showed above the level of the barrens. Here they halted, and Darling whistled guardedly. An answering note came up to them from the blackness below and to seaward. Darling stepped down, parted the young birches and twisted alders with one arm and drew Flora into the cover. She stumbled, saved herself from falling by encountering his broad chest – and then she put up both arms and slipped them about his neck.

"My God! Do you mean it, Flora?" he whispered.

For answer, her arms tightened about his neck. He lowered his head slowly, staring at the pale oval of her face – and so their lips met.

Another cautious whistle from below brought them to a realization of their surroundings. They continued their downward journey and presently found George Wick. George was in a bad humor. He was cold, and he grumbled in cautious growls.

"So ye come for a girl, did ye? Well, there bes another girl in this harbor I'd like to be fetchin' away wid me! Aye, here she bes now, wid the bully."

Mary sprang ashore.

"Here ye be. Git yer gear aboard quick, an' away wid ye," she whispered, "an' don't forget yer promise."

"I'll be comin' back for ye, one o' these days," said George Wick.

"Then ye needn't, for ye bain't wanted," replied Mary.

John and Flora scarcely heard her; but George gave ear until the last swish and rustle of her ascent through the brush died away. Then he fell to loading the bully. Five minutes later they took their places aboard, pushed out of the little cove, stepped the mast and spread the red sail.

Flora sat in the stern-sheets. John managed the tiller with his left hand. The light breeze wafted them northward. At last George Wick broke the silence.

"Hark! What bes that?" he exclaimed.

"It sounded like gun-shots," said John, indifferently.

"I suppose that mad skipper is fighting with his men," said Flora – and the breath of her words touched the sailor's cheek.

B LACK DENNIS NOLAN and Bill Brennen brought the loose jewels from their hiding-place to the harbor. The skipper carried the dispatch-box, and in his pockets he had John Darling's neat little pistols, each good for two shots – the latest thing in pistols at that time. They went straight to Cornelius Lynch's cabin, where the leading grumblers were assembled. The skipper was about to kick open the door and stuff the jewels into their insatiable maws when a guarded, anxious voice at his elbow arrested him with one foot drawn back. The voice was that of Mary Kavanagh.

"Whist!" said Mary. "Bes that yerself, Denny Nolan?"

"Aye, sure it be," returned the skipper.

"I heard a sound on the cliff, to the north," said Mary. "The sound o' a horse nickerin' an' men cursin' it for the same."

"A horse?" queried the skipper. And then, "On the cliff to the north? Where the divil has ye been to, Mary Kavanagh?"

"Whist! Hark to that!" exclaimed the girl.

"Sure, skipper, 'twas somethin' up back yonder," whispered Bill Brennen. "It sounded to meself like a gun slammin' agin a rock."

"Would it be that stranger lad?" queried Dennis, anxiously.

"Nay, he bes safe enough," said Mary. "But hark to that, now! There bes a whole crew up yonder."

The skipper opened Cornelius Lynch's door, but not with his foot as he had formerly intended.

"Turn out an' git yer guns, men. There bes trouble a-foot," he said, quietly. Then, laying a hand on Mary's shoulder, he whispered, "Git Pat an' yerself to my house an' fasten up the doors. It bes a strong house, lass, an' if there bes any gunnin' ye'll be safe there."

"Ye needn't be worryin' for Flora Lockhart," said Mary. "She bes safe enough – herself an' the captain – a-sailing away in the bully this half-hour back."

The skipper's hand tightened on her shoulder; but she did not flinch. In the light from the open door he stared at her – and she stared back at him, glance for glance. There was astonishment in his eyes rather than anger, and a question rather than condemnation. He was about to speak when the smashing report of a musket rang out from the slope and a slug splintered the edge of the open door. The skipper pushed Mary away from him.

"Run! Run to the house!" he cried.

Mary vanished into the darkness. Men clustered around the skipper, sealing-guns, pistols, cutlasses and clubs in their hands, their grumblings forgotten in the prospect of a fight. The open door was shut with a bang.

"Follow me!" shouted the skipper, dropping the dispatch-box of loose jewels to the trampled snow and pulling his pistols from his pocket.

The men of Chance Along and Pierre Benoist's ruffians met at the foot of the steep slope, among the upper rank of cabins. All doubts as to the intentions of the visitors were dispelled from the skipper's mind by a voice shouting, "Git inside the houses, lads, an' pull up the floors. There bes where ye'll find the stuff. Git into the big house. *It* be fair full o' gold an' jewels."

The voice was that of Dick Lynch. The skipper knew it, and his pistols flashed and banged in his hands.

The light of the stars, dimmed by a high, thin veil of mist, was not good enough to fight scientifically by. After the first clash it was almost impossible to know friend from foe at the length of an arm. Single combats, and cursing knots of threes and fours, staggered and swatted among the little dwellings. The work was entirely too close for gun-work, and so the weapons were clubbed and the affair hammered out like hot irons on an anvil.

After ten minutes of it the skipper found himself in front of his own door, with a four-foot stick of green birch in his hands, and something wet and warm trickling from his forehead into his left eye. Three men were at him. Bill McKay was one of them and Pierre Benoist another. McKay fought with a clubbed musket, and the French sailor held a dirk in one hand and an empty pistol in the other. The third prodded about in the background with a cutlass. He seemed to be of a retiring disposition.

The skipper defended his position heroically; but after two minutes of it the musket proved heavier than the club of birch, and he received a crack on his left shoulder that put one arm out of action. The Frenchman ducked and slipped in; but the skipper's boot on his collar-bone set him back for a moment and sent the knife tinkling to the ground. But the same movement, thanks to the little wad of snow on the heel of his boot, brought the skipper to the flat of his back with a bone-shaking slam. The clubbed musket swung up – and then the door flew open above his upturned face, candle-light flooded over him and a sealing-gun flashed and bellowed. Then the threatening musket fell of its own weight, from dead hands – and the skipper went to sleep with more stars twirling white and green fire across his inner vision than he had ever seen in the sky.

It was daylight when Black Dennis Nolan next opened his eyes. He was in his own bed. He felt very sick in the stomach, very light in the head, very dry in the mouth. Old Mother Nolan sat beside the bed, smoking her pipe.

"Was it ye let off the old gun out the door?" he asked.

"Nay, 'twas Mary done it," replied Mother Nolan, blinking her black eyes at him.

"An' where bes Mary now?" he asked.

"In me own bed. Sure, when she was draggin' ye into the house, didn't some divil jab her in the neck wid a great knife."

The skipper sat up, though the effort spun a purple haze across his eyes, and set a lump of red-hot iron knocking about inside his skull.

"Bes she – dead?" he whispered.

"Nay, lad, nay, she bain't what ye'd call dead," replied the old woman.

The skipper rolled to the floor, scrambled to his feet, reeled across the kitchen and into the next room, and sank at the side of Mary's bed. He was done. He could not lift himself an inch higher; but a hand came down to him, over the side of the bed, and touched his battered brow.

A week later, Mary Kavanagh was able to sit up in Mother Nolan's bed; and the skipper was himself again, at least as far as the cut over his eye and the bump on top of his head were concerned.

The skipper and Mother Nolan sat by Mary's bed. The skipper looked older, wiser and less sure of himself than in the brisk days before the raid.

"I bes a poor man now," he said. "Sure, them robbers broke t'rough this harbor somethin' desperate! Didn't the back o' the chimley look like the divil had been a-clawin' it out?"

"Quick come and quick go! Ye bes lucky, lad, they didn't sail away wid yer fore-an'-after," said Mother Nolan.

"Aye, Granny; but it do beat me how ever they come to dig up the kitchen-floor."

"Sure, an' they didn't," said Mary. " 'Twas meself done that — an' sent the red an' white diamonds away wid Flora's man. 'Twas himself ye took 'em from, Denny Nolan."

"An' a good thing, too,' said Mother Nolan. "Sure, ye sent all the curses o' Chance Along away together, Mary dear! There bain't no luck in wracked gold, nor wracked diamonds — nor wracked women! Grub an' gear bes our right; but not gold an' humans."

The skipper gazed at the girl until her eyes met his.

"Was ye workin' agin me all the time?" he asked, quietly.

"Nay, Denny, but I was workin' *for* ye — all the time," she whispered.

"Sure she was," said Mother Nolan, puffing at her pipe. "Aye — an' many's the time 'twas on me tongue to call her a fool for her trouble, ye was that bewitched an' bemazed, lad."

The skipper stared at the floor for a long time, in silence. At last he said, "Wid the way ye was workin', Mary, the wonder bes to me what for ye risked the knife in yer neck to save me life from the Frenchman."

"Denny, ye bes still a fool!" exclaimed Mother Nolan. "When you bain't one manner o' fool ye bes another! What for! d'ye ask! Well, what for?"

"Sure, I was only wonderin'," said the man, glancing shyly and hopefully at the girl in the bed.

Father McQueen reached Chance Along early in June. He found plenty of work awaiting him, including six masses for the newly-dead, and the building of the church. The general tone of the harbor impressed him as being strangely subdued. Even Black Dennis Nolan seemed less vivid and dominant in his bearing; but in spite of this change in him, he refused to put off his wedding even for the glory of being married in the new church.

In spite of a scar on her round, white neck, Mary Nolan was the grandest-looking, sweetest bride that had ever been seen in Chance Along. Denny thought so, and old Barney Keen said it, and Mother Nolan proved it by admitting that even she herself had not cut such a figure, under similar circumstances, fifty years ago. And on the morning after the wedding, the skipper and Mary set out on their honeymoon to St. John's, aboard the fore-and-after, with a freight of salvaged cargo under the hatch instead of thiefed jewels and gold. Back in the harbor the men unmoored their skiffs for the fishing, even as their fathers had done since the first Nolan and the first Leary spied that coast. They grumbled a little, as was their nature; but there was no talk of mutiny or treason. The red tide of greed had ebbed away with the passing of the sense of possession, and the fear of bewitchment had faded away with the departure of the innocent witch.

∞

THE AUTHOR

Theodore Goodridge Roberts came of a family which for generations had taken an interest in literary and scholarly matters. In his own generation, it was particularly well represented in the creative arts, since Sir Charles G. D. Roberts was his brother, and Bliss Carman his cousin. Theodore was born in 1877 in Fredericton, New Brunswick, the fifth child of the Reverend George Goodridge Roberts. He was educated in Fredericton, and in 1897 went to New York, to become sub-editor of the magazine *The Independent*, for which he became correspondent during the Spanish-American war. Although during the ensuing years he was to live in many parts of the world, Fredericton remained the hub of his existence and it was to Fredericton he always returned. He died in 1953 and is buried in that city's Forest Hill Cemetery.

His long and productive literary career included thirty-four novels, four books of verse, and well over a hundred short stories. His historical romances and adventure stories (for both adults and children) are set in Newfoundland, the woods of New Brunswick, in Central America and on the high seas. Many were first published in magazines, appearing later in book form. His familiarity with the attitudes and speech patterns of the coast dwellers of Newfoundland is reflected in both his prose and his verse. His works include *The House of Issens* (1900); *Hemming, the Adventurer* (1904); *Brothers in Peril* (1905); *Red Feathers* (1907); *Captain Love* (1908); *A Cavalier of Virginia* (1910); *A Captain of Raleigh's* (1911); *The Wasp* (1914). *Seven Poems* was published in 1925, *The Lost Shipmate* in 1926 and a book of his collected verse, *The Leather Bottle*, in 1934.

THE NEW CANADIAN LIBRARY